LITTLE BOAT BOY

LITTLE BOAT BOY

A Story of Kashmir

by JEAN BOTHWELL

ILLUSTRATED BY MARGARET AYER

HARCOURT, BRACE & WORLD, INC. · NEW YORK

TO JIMMIE

Who Once Was Eight

CONTENTS

CONTENTS

LITTLE BOAT BOY

CHARACTERS

Hafiz—a boy of Kashmir

His family—Father
              Mother
              Brother Abdullah
              Sister Rafia

Sayyad Khan—a rug merchant and moneylender

The wood-carver

The farmer

His wife and their baby

The farmer's coolie and his wife

Yusuf Ali—school friend of Abdullah

The Sahib—an English artist

1

HAFIZ WAITS FOR SPRING

THE FLEET OF TINY BOATS CAME SLOWLY IN
to dock under the arching root of a willow tree.
The root and the bank made a perfect bay for
them. The small boy who guided their course
with a long stick looked at each one lovingly.
No two were alike.

One boat was only a chip of walnut wood,

which he had found in the shavings at the wood-carver's shop. But it looked like a freight barge to the boy because he had tied on a cargo of willow twigs.

Another was made from the halves of a walnut shell, fastened together with a shred of leather from the long curling end at the tip of his shoe. His mother had not yet noticed that he had cut it off. In one half of the shell boat stood a sturdy sailor made from pine needles which had once blown in the winds on Solomon's Mountain.

There was a miniature *doonga*, too, like the one in which Hafiz himself lived, with a wide deck in front and a mat-enclosed shelter for the family. The wood-carver in the bazaar, who made them for tourists, had given him that one for the sake of an errand well performed. There should be a little houseboat like the big one his father rented to summer visitors. It was possible to buy them, but he had no coppers.

He gave the small *shikara* an extra push. It was the last to stop against the root. Grandfather had carved it, even making two heart-shaped paddles like the big ones used on the lake. His mother had found a bit of cloth in her stores box for the tiny curtains and a cushion for the seat. Only Hafiz knew that the seat could be taken out. He had not yet named the *shikara*, though it is the custom in Kashmir to give each *shikara* a name of its own. He must find a name.

The whole family had tried to help but nothing they liked had suited him. The big ones on hire at Dal Gate had beautiful names, with flowers and birds in them. But Hafiz steadily refused to have any name he had yet heard. He wanted to think of one himself.

Each boat had its own painter, a piece of

bright red wool which the owner of the shawl shop at Third Bridge had not needed. At least, it had been bright when new. Many tyings and untyings and frequent dips in the water had dulled the lovely color, but the strands of wool were still firm.

Hafiz scarcely breathed while he fastened each boat carefully in its own place under the willow root. Then he sat back on his heels, to look at his treasures. He stretched his outer coat down over his feet until he looked like a little button mushroom that had suddenly sprouted at the edge of the water. He wore several coats, one on top of the other, all cut alike in a shapeless fashion of wide sleeves and ankle-length baggy comfort. The soft wool material, spun and woven in the town, had kept him warm all winter.

It did not matter to Hafiz that his clothes were dirty. The smoke from the cooking fire, many splashings from lake and river water, all the spots of grease from luscious bygone curry, had spoiled the freshness of his clothes when they were new. But he did not mind, nor did anyone. Everybody looked the same and for the same reasons.

The small skull-fitting cap on the back of Hafiz' head, covering his short hair, looked like a shiny piece of round leather. It had once been new cloth like his coats, embroidered in a gay pattern. But the embroidery had worn off, and weather and wear had changed the color. It was a warm cap and that was enough.

The boats rode quietly under the willow root. Hafiz leaned down and dipped a finger in the water, then held it up in the air. But there was still no breeze to dry his grubby little brown hand. There had been no wind all afternoon. He was sure, though, that the water was almost warm. Spring was a little bit here, he thought happily, squinting up at the clear sky through the pale mist of new leaves on the willow tree. The thin sunlight felt good on his face.

The mushroom became a boy again, as Hafiz stretched out contentedly on the low bank. He lay as still as water and earth and sky. They, too, waited for spring.

The *doonga* and the small houseboat it served were moored near a narrow runway of land with a line of willow trees for shade. In the channel between the runway and the lake bank a family of ducks were feeding on water plants. They made pleasant soft sounds as they moved slowly about.

From the other side of the willows which hid Hafiz, he could hear his mother and older sister, Rafia, talking. They were out on the runway husking rice in a hollowed-out log. The thump, thump, thump of the heavy wooden pestle made little dashes between their words.

On much higher ground, beyond the end of the runway, a farmer and his coolie were preparing a field. Hafiz had watched them set out cabbage plants earlier in the day. Now they were drawing water from the lake. A tall frame, two uprights and a crossbeam, on a stout platform extending over the lake, held a pulley. A large round water jar with a wide mouth was let down into the water. It came back brimming full and shining. The wet clay was bright red in the sunlight. The coolie hauled it up, hand over hand, on the rope slung through the pulley. Then he poured the water from the jar into the little ditches between the rows of plants. He sang a few clear notes when he let the rope down, and repeated them as he brought the glistening jar up to the level of the field.

The lilting melody of the well-song, chanted over and over again, was caught between the heavy thumps of the rice-husking and the soft chatter of the ducks. It was a good sound, a homey sound to Hafiz.

The little boy pushed the loose sleeve of his outer coat up under his cheek, closed his eyes and became even more a part of the subdued waiting about him, the stillness of early spring.

In summer Kashmir is a bright land where cherries grow and children play in the water all day long. Its ancient valley is walled in by snow-capped mountains. Its people are a fair race, strong in body and accustomed to simple living.

Some of the people are farmers, who grow vegetables along Dal Lake in Srinagar City, or on the many floating garden islands in the lake. Their families are sheltered in bleak-looking, unpainted wooden houses which stand on high foundations above the marshy ground.

But many Kashmiris never know any other home than a mat house on a freight barge—that, or the *doonga* trailing behind a houseboat. Those who live in the town make beautiful things with their hands, in wool and wood and silk and silver.

When spring comes the farmers sing and the wood-carvers open their loft doors to let in the lovely sunshine. In summer, iris and poppies bloom in the thatch on the bare houses and flower petals float on the water.

Tourists come from far away, and again and again, to live in the houseboats on lake and river, eat the cherries, paint the snows, and buy the famous carvings and embroideries.

It is a picturesque country, that lovely Valley. But Hafiz was not too young to have learned some homely things. Plain, true things. He knew that if many visitors came in summer, times were easier in winter. He knew, if there were a season when the black sickness—cholera—was bad, and the houseboats were not rented, there would be hunger in his Valley. Then the people must borrow money from the lender in the bazaar to buy food.

All winter he had hoped that the coming season would be good and that their boat would be rented quickly. He would be so glad for spring to come. Then they would know.

2

THE FAMILY MAKES PLANS

THE BOOM OF THE EVENING GUN AT THE
Fort woke Hafiz. The sun was low and he was
cold. The farmer and his coolie had gone home.
The ducks were clustered all in one spot, getting ready for the night. The women had carried their husking log back to the *doonga*.

Now, at the cooking place inside the mat-enclosed stern, the flames of the supper fire leaped around the rice pot. Rafia crouched in front of the low fireplace, raking the coals into an even bed. The warmth and comfort there drew Hafiz almost against his will into the family group. He was hungry and the smell of supper was very good.

The first evening star had appeared above Solomon's Mountain. The little boy watched for it every night and every night it seemed larger. He stopped with one foot on land and the other on the short plank which led to the bow of the *doonga*. He looked about him. Just ahead the quiet houseboat lay, moving gently as the evening wind, rising, blew little waves across the lake.

Hafiz lifted his face to the deepening blue above him. Did the wind begin up there with the stars? He supposed that boys who went to school knew all about the stars and the wind and boats. Abdullah had gone to the River School. He wished that he, too, might go.

The great mass of the rugged hill made a darker patch on the water beyond the house-boat. Many stars began to appear in the patch as Hafiz stood watching. He wondered again who would live in their boat this year. Would anyone want it? The renting season would begin when spring came.

He stooped and put his finger in the water again. It was very cold. How long must they wait? Perhaps, if they had a good season, there would be enough money for school fees.

From her place by the fire, Hafiz' mother turned to look out the doorway, where the mat was still rolled up. The others at the sides and end had been pulled down snugly over the frame to keep the wind out for the night. Hafiz heard her call to him.

"Come in, boy! Why do you stand in the cold? Thy father has come and the coals are red. Come in to thy food and sleep! Hear me!"

Hafiz slowly set his other foot on the plank. He did not want to go in, and started to say so, but a huge yawn drowned the words. And the supper smelled very good.

When he came into the light of the fire, he found his father and Abdullah, his tall brother, already settled in a corner of the cooking place. He wished he had not been asleep beyond the willow trees when Abdullah came home. He liked watching the big boy paddle the *shikara* up to the *doonga,* leap out of the long narrow boat and fasten it almost in one motion. It was fun to see him stride across the open end of the *doonga* and suddenly bend down to enter the mat shelter. He, Hafiz, did not have to bend. Would he ever get to be as tall as Abdullah? Did going to school make one grow tall?

Abdullah had been talking to his father, but he stopped when he saw Hafiz and said: "Ho there, small owner of mighty boats! Is the fleet in for the night?"

Hafiz blinked in the firelight and smiled, sleepily.

"Come, see what I have brought you!"

Abdullah drew the little boy to a place beside him in the corner and from an inner fold of his clothing produced a small object which he put in Hafiz' hand. Hafiz leaned nearer the firelight to see. A lantern had been lighted and hung from one of the uprights of the mat frame, but the firelight was brighter.

The family watched him. Rafia moved the rice pot and the glow from the red coals shone on a tiny clay figurine, exactly the length of his little finger. Hafiz knew the shop where it had been made. It was near First Bridge. He had passed it once with his father but he had had no coppers.

Now his big brother had brought him a soldier in the Kashmir uniform. Why had Abdullah gone to First Bridge? A recruiting office was there, near the Palace! Was that where he had gone?

Rafia saw what the little toy was, and said "Oh!", as if something hurt her very much. She looked at Abdullah. Hafiz knew that the father and mother looked at each other, hard, and that the father shook his head. He, himself, turned to Abdullah. He salaamed first, both little hands, palms together, at his forehead. That was for thanks. Then, he too looked at Abdullah gravely, until the older boy laughed and shook his head as their father had done.

Abdullah was not going away to the Fort then. For many weeks an argument had gone on hotly between Abdullah and his father, Hafiz knew. All the family had heard it. Abdullah wanted to be a soldier in the State Army and their father had said "No!" thunderously.

The big bearded man was not often so stern. He had added that if going to school gave boys such ideas, then no other member of his family should be allowed to go. Furthermore, Abdullah was needed to help earn the family living. Some other boy would have to be hired to serve the table in the houseboat if Abdullah joined the Army. It did not matter that he could be an officer.

That thunderous "No!" had echoed in Hafiz' ears for a long time. And he tried not to think about the rest of it, that no other member of the family could go to school. It could only mean himself, for girls did not go to school. They stayed at home and helped their mothers.

Out of the small silence about the fire, the father spoke from his shadowy corner. "What will you do with your soldier, Small One?"

Hafiz looked down at the clay figure. "He will ride in the *shikara* very grandly, under the curtains, my father," said the little boy, respectfully. Then he looked at Abdullah and smiled.

The big brother had been watching for that sign of joy. Hafiz' smile was not an ordinary grin. When he was happy, and that was most of the time, it was as if someone had lighted a candle behind his deep-set brown eyes. His whole face glowed. That was all the reward Abdullah wanted.

Abdullah settled Hafiz comfortably in the corner beside him and the mother began to serve the hot food. She and Rafia would wait until their menfolk had eaten before taking their own portions.

Tonight there was lamb curry with the rice. Hafiz ate quickly, rolling the rice into little balls with his fingers, to dip up the spicy meat gravy. While he ate, the soldier stood at his side on the floor of the boat. When his bowl was empty, Rafia took it and Hafiz listened to the talk which had begun again between his father and Abdullah.

Some day, perhaps, his father would talk to him in the same way, if he were allowed to go to school. He was big enough now, truly. Abdullah was almost a man, and he himself was eight whole years old.

There had been a letter that day. It had come from the artist Sahib who had lived in their houseboat last summer. Abdullah read the letter aloud, for all to hear. The Sahib wanted to rent their boat again this season!

He would be coming up from India early, he wrote, and he hoped they could let him know by the next post. If they let him have the boat, would they please tie up in the same place as last summer? He would send the money for the fee.

So, Hafiz thought, while he had been asleep beyond the willows and while he was coming in to supper, the letter had lain there in Abdullah's pocket. They did not need to wait for spring to know that the boat would be rented. Everything would be all right now. They were already in the place they had been last year. He sighed, out loud, for relief, and the others looked round at him, but went on talking when he said nothing.

The warm food and the fire had made Hafiz very sleepy but he fought it for a while. He hated to go to sleep now. He wanted to ask Abdullah about the recruiting office, if he had been there, and what the man had said. Of course Abdullah could not go in the Army if the Sahib was coming. He was a very nice man. He had lived alone in the houseboat and did not bother them for extra things all the

22

time. The talk in the bazaar had it that some tenants were never pleased.

On and on went the family discussion. The mother and Rafia were in it, too, planning for the new season. They said the houseboat should be cleaned. Abdullah and his father did not think so. Because they would have to do it, Hafiz suspected. He chuckled, but nobody heard, they were arguing so hard.

Hafiz could not stay awake any longer. His eyes would not stay open. He fell over suddenly. His head hit the smooth walnut floor boards with a loud thump. It hurt! He lay where he fell for a minute. His mother came over to him and shook him, gently. All her silver ornaments jingled when she moved. The many bracelets on her arms and the heavier anklets made a little tune. Hafiz loved that sound.

"Come, Small One! Now is the time for sleep. See, thy soldier will sleep too!" She picked up the little clay toy and put it in Hafiz' hand. He stood up slowly and followed her to the other side of the fire where Rafia had unrolled a cotton-filled mat, thicker than those woven of rushes which covered the roof frame. He lay down in his many coats and his mother covered him with a warm wadded quilt which he pulled up over his head.

The quilt shut out the light but he could feel the gentle pushes the lake gave the boat. The water made a slap pat sound against the sides. He could hear it, even through the heavy folds of his covering.

Now that he was shut away from the air, the spicy odor of the curry was strong again. He had not washed his hands. He rubbed them along the front of his coat. It was a wonderful smell. They had not had meat for a long time, but with a tenant promised for the houseboat, they could have meat again. And Abdullah was not going away! He was sorry for Abdullah, but he was a little glad their father had said that "No!"

Tomorrow he, Hafiz, would guide the fleet out into the garden channel again and give the new soldier a ride. He felt for the little toy. It had slipped out of his hand and was lying beyond the quilt, on the floor. Hafiz sat up and stood him securely in a crack where the floor and boat wall joined.

When he lay down again, he felt the lake pushing the boat a little harder. The wind was rising. He threw back a corner of his quilt to see if a storm were coming. Perhaps he should have brought the little boats in for the night. But someone had rolled down the mat at the door and the lantern had been put out. The time for sleep had come for the whole family.

3

HAFIZ EATS BREAKFAST

THE NEXT MORNING THE COCOON BY THE fire that was Hafiz stirred late. He came out of his quilt to find the mats still fastened down. There had been a storm in the night. Only Rafia was in sight, and she was making flat cakes of bread at the fire.

She smiled at him and waved the bread tongs. "So, little brother!" she said. "You are a fine fellow indeed. The day is begun. You should be out, tending the little boats."

Hafiz grinned and held out his hand for bread.

Rafia shook her head. "Nay! Remember what the Sahib said last summer?"

She dropped into the ashes the flat round of bread she had just taken off the fire. It puffed up into a ball before going flat again, moist with its own steam. How good it smelled!

"Teeth!" said Rafia, making a brisk rubbing motion with her hand. "Do I have to say it every morning?"

Hafiz might sleep in his clothes. He could go to bed without washing his hands. But his teeth were another matter. They shone against his olive skin like big grains of rice. Rafia had told him over and over that he must keep them that way.

The little boy sat in his quilt awhile, getting awake. Rafia went on making bread. That was her work. For every meal Rafia made fresh bread. Hafiz watched her slim hands, rolling the dough and patting it flat, on the small round pastry board which stood up off the floor on three little knobs.

"If I could go to school, Rafia, I could count the bread," said Hafiz, with a wide yawn.

Rafia fluttered her fingers at him. "Who wants it counted? It tastes just as good. Abdullah can teach you to count, and you can stay here with us. One schoolboy in the family is enough."

Hafiz sighed. First his father, and now Rafia. He had better change the subject.

"Where is my father?"

"He has gone to the tax office, to get the renting paper."

"Where is my mother?"

"She went with thy father as far as the wood-carver's house. They have a new baby."

28

"My wood-carver? The one that gave me the boat? I carried his basket for him."

"Yes, little coolie, thy wood-carver. They've got a very new little boy. Today is his name day."

"What will his name be?"

"The same as your own."

Hafiz thought about that for a while. Rafia went on with the bread.

"I wish we had a baby, Rafia. I would tend him. I would play with him. But he couldn't have my name. That is mine. How can that other baby have my name?"

"Lots of people have the same name. But not in the same family. You are our baby, so, our baby is Hafiz. And the wood-carver can have one Hafiz, too!"

Rafia laughed, and Hafiz chuckled, way down in his tummy. Rafia was such a funny sister. He was not a baby now. She had forgot he was eight years old.

He listened a moment, quietly. He could not hear Abdullah. He and Rafia must be alone in the boat.

"Where is my brother?"

"He has gone to the post office to send the letter to the Sahib."

Rafia put her rolling pin and the little pastry board in the stores box. She set the basket of bread by the fire and covered it with a square of cloth.

"Now then, Hafiz!" Even if Rafia were only fourteen, she could talk like their mother sometimes, and Hafiz knew that tone.

Through the open door blew the fresh smell that comes after a hard rain. Bruised new willow leaves were in it, wet mats and low-hanging smoke. But the sun was out, gloriously, and the world had a shining look.

Hafiz stretched his head out, away from the

quilt, and sniffed. Suddenly he sprang up, found his cap, thrust his feet into the small shoes with pointed tips and dashed outdoors. He heard Rafia follow him to the door but he did not look back.

From the first willow tree on the bank he broke off a tender shoot and stripped it of leaves. One end he put in his mouth and crushed it with his shiny white teeth. When the fiber was separated and flat he went back to the boat, where his sister was waiting for him, as he knew she would be. It was the same every morning.

Rafia leaned down and dropped a small piece of charcoal in his hand. Hafiz stooped and dipped the willow brush in the lake. He was ready to clean his teeth with the charcoal.

While he worked, a kingfisher came and sat on the peak of the roof. His wings looked a deeper blue against the dark brown rush mats. Hafiz went on brushing. Suddenly there was a whirr and a blue flash and the kingfisher dived. He had been searching in the clear space at the end of the boat for his breakfast. He shot downward and came up with a small fish in his beak. The water showered behind in a crystal fall as he flew away. Hafiz sat back on his heels to watch the bird and Rafia went inside.

In a moment there was a call from the cooking place. "Here is breakfast for you, too, boatman!"

The willow brush was tossed in the lake. Hafiz' pointed shoes made two steps up the plank, two steps to the door, one to the fire. He held out both hands. Rafia laid a hot flat round of bread on them. It shone with the fat she had spread on it. Melting in the fat in the center was brown sugar, shaved from the great round cake of it which the mother kept in the stores box.

Hafiz walked carefully outdoors, sliding his

feet along the polished floor boards so as not to spill one precious grain of the sugar. He did not have sugar on his bread every morning. He sat down slowly against the side of the boat, waiting for the bread to cool a little. He did not want to burn his tongue.

All about him the world was glowing. Spring was much nearer. The sun felt warmer on his face today. The farmer and his coolie were working among the plants in the high field. Ahead, there was a blue and white and green picture on the water. A row of poplar trees on the opposite bank made it, upside down against the snow ranges and the blue northern sky.

Inside, Rafia was moving about and he knew she was rolling up quilts and mats and heaping all of them in one corner for the day. That was her work, too.

Hafiz sat there a long time, eating the bread and sugar. He broke off each bit very gently and chewed and chewed. When the bread was quite finished, he noticed a few sugar crumbs had fallen on the boat floor. He wet the tip of one finger with his tongue and picked up all the crumbs. Then he licked the sugar rim from his mouth. There was nothing left.

He walked to the other end of the boat to look for the returning family. No one was in sight, anywhere. He leaned way over the side of the boat to touch the tips of his fingers in the lake water. He had had breakfast. Now he would see if the water was cold or warm and clean his hands at the same time. After that he could go to see his little boats and give the soldier a ride in the *shikara*.

The next moment he was in the water, all of him! He yelled. Rafia ran outdoors. The farmer and his coolie came to the edge of the field. Rafia shouted to them and pointed toward Hafiz. He saw her mouth very wide open as he

went down. When he came up, beating the water with his hands and sputtering, the *doonga* looked very far away and the sloping stern very high.

He felt something beside him in the water. It hit his shoulder. There, red and wet, floated the big clay jar which the coolie used for drawing water. The farmer was waving his arms and calling something, over and over again. Hafiz stopped yelling to listen, while he grasped the edge of the water jar with both hands.

"Get in, baby! Get in the jar! We will help you! Get in! Get in!"

Hafiz understood. "But I'm not a baby," he insisted aloud, and clung more tightly to the edge of the only solid thing in reach. "And I don't want to get into this jar."

Rafia was screaming something at him, too, while she rushed frantically from one side of the boat to the other. The ducks had set up a terrific quacking. Some people passing in a taxi-boat stopped to see what was causing all the noise. Then they started to pull in toward the lake bank. Hafiz saw them coming. They would take him into that strange boat. It would be better to get in the jar.

So he tugged on the rope and managed to get his knee over the edge. He almost fell back into the lake again because the jar tilted. But when he got one foot inside, it leveled. It was easier then to pull up the other foot and stand upright. The coolie started to haul him up so suddenly that he would even then have had another dip in the lake had he not grasped the rope in time. He stood very still while the coolie and the farmer together drew the swaying jar up to the top and over to the land.

They lifted him out and he remembered Rafia down there in the *doonga*. He waved to her and she promptly sat down and began to cry.

Hafiz was very wet. All his coats dripped and dripped. The farmer laughed and Hafiz laughed, too. Then he sneezed. The farmer said something, sharply, to the coolie. The man dropped the rope he was still holding and hurried to the edge of the platform. He shouted to Rafia. There was an answer, but the voice was Abdullah's.

Abdullah was back from his errand! Hafiz followed the coolie. When he reached the platform he held the man's hand, so he would not fall in the water again. The coolie was talking to Abdullah.

A little ring of drops from the hem of his coats tickled Hafiz' feet. His shoes were lost in the lake, and his feet were muddy from standing in the field. He began to shake with cold. He stood first on one foot, then the other, trying to dry them and stop the queer tickling feeling, but the water dripped and dripped. It wasn't so funny now.

Hafiz looked down. Below them Abdullah sat in a *shikara* without any top, and it was drawn quite close to the lake bank. The friend who had brought him home pushed one of his paddles into the bank and held the boat still.

Abdullah looked up at Hafiz. "Ho, sailor! I have come to take you home. If you get in the water jar again and come down, I will lift you out and into this boat."

Hafiz shook his head and sneezed again. The coolie and Abdullah talked some more. The little boy looked at the clay water jar. He remembered how the rope had felt in his hands. It was strong. It had carried him to the top. But the men had pulled. It had come up slowly. This time he would be going the other way. Would they hold the rope or let him go too fast? If they let the jar down fast he would surely fall in the water once more.

The farmer joined them and Hafiz stood in the middle, holding onto a hand of each man. It was easier to stand on one foot and try to dry the other that way. Then Abdullah stood up in the boat. He showed Hafiz two coppers, one in each hand.

"A copper, Hafiz! For coming down! And this one, my boatman, for going up!"

Hafiz started to shake his head again. But a wonderful new idea came into his mind, a reason for doing many hard things perhaps. He forgot he was cold and scared. His eyes sparkled. He laughed, showing all his white teeth. He dropped the men's hands and stepped over to the water jar. The coolie and the farmer came too. They looked at the rope where it ran over the pulley in the frame. It was strong. It would carry Hafiz down. The farmer wrapped the rope around his arm and walked back onto the field a little way. The coolie helped Hafiz get into the jar. He lifted it out over the water. The frame creaked. Hafiz said "Oh!" just once, but very loud.

Quite slowly, twisting around a little, but certainly going down, the jar carried the little boy to meet Abdullah. Beyond the *shikara* he could see Rafia watching from the *doonga*. He could see the ducks, too, in their pool beyond the willows. The silly things! They were still rushing back and forth on the water and quacking loudly.

Beneath him, Abdullah stretched up his arms and caught the edge of the water jar to steady it. Then Hafiz was beside Abdullah on the seat of the boat and the coolie was pulling the empty jar up again.

Hafiz' clothes dripped all over the *shikara* seat, but Yusuf, Abdullah's friend, did not mind. There were no cushions to be spoiled. It was only a plain *shikara*. Abdullah said, "Fine, Yusuf! We are ready." Yusuf said, "Very good!" and took his paddle out of the lake bank.

Abdullah held Hafiz very tightly and put the two coppers in his hand. Hafiz smiled.

From the bank of the lake below the field to the *doonga* was only a short distance when one was not in the water. Rafia drew the little dripping figure into the warmth of the fireplace. Abdullah came too, while Yusuf waited outside. Together, the brother and sister stripped the little boy's clothes off and wrapped him in his quilt on his mat.

Then Hafiz remembered. "My shoes, Rafia!" He began to cry for the first time since he fell in the water. "My shoes are lost in the lake!"

Rafia was gathering up the little heap of soggy clothes. She had been crying, too. She sniffed and said "Shoes!" as if they did not matter. But his shoes did matter, very much.

He had no others. Abdullah said, "Never mind, perhaps we shall find them!"

Abdullah had been to school and Rafia had not. Abdullah knew that shoes were important.

It wasn't night, but Hafiz felt as if it were. Of course the sun would not be shining at night. Here it was, coming in through the cracks where the mats on the roof had shifted. It made patterns on the floor. The patterns moved when the water pushed the boat.

Hafiz watched them a little while, after Rafia and Abdullah had gone away. It was very nice to be warm and safely back on his own boat. His eyes felt heavy, the same as they did at night, and the dancing light hurt them. That was because he had cried. He turned over on his side, toward the wall.

There, in the crack of the floor where Hafiz had put him, was the little soldier. He had been standing in it all night and all morning. It was then Hafiz remembered that he had not yet gone to see his little boats. He laid his two coppers at the soldier's feet.

"Guard my money well, soldier!" he said. "Tomorrow you shall have a ride in a very grand *shikara*."

4

THE FARMER LOSES
AN ARGUMENT

HAFIZ DREAMED THAT THE LITTLE SOLDIER climbed out of the crack and played with the coppers. They rolled against each other with a little tinkle and the soldier laughed.

But when Hafiz opened his eyes, the soldier stood primly in his place and the little boy knew the sound had really been the sweet jingle of his mother's anklets. She was outside with his father and they were talking. Abdullah was there, too. So, it was afternoon and the name day party was over. Had they brought him any sweets?

Hafiz lay still, blinking at the light and re-membering. A great deal had happened that day. He wanted to get up now. He yawned, a very loud one, so that somebody would hear and come to him. It was rather nice, once in a while, to be the family baby.

Nobody came. He tried it again. This time Rafia heard but she got only as far as the door. She whispered, "Sshh! Sshh! Hafiz!" and laid her finger on her lips. Then she stood there, looking out.

The talk outside was growing louder. Hafiz raised himself on one elbow to listen. Another voice grew clear. It was the farmer's. What did he want?

The tune of the anklets and bracelets had changed to a jerky clashing. His mother was having a part in an argument! Her tone was shrill. She said something about the farmer's family. Hafiz grinned. He had heard that often. A fight always made people say things about each other's relatives.

His father was saying, "Nay!" and "Nay!" and "Nay!", in the same way, gently but with meaning, every time the farmer stopped for breath. The farmer seemed very angry about something.

"Rafia, why is the farmer . . . ?"

Rafia turned and laid her finger on her lips again. "Hush, little brother!"

It was then Hafiz saw his clothes in her hand. He leaped out of the quilt and ran to her. Rafia pulled him back to the quilt, away from the door. She began to help him dress. The clothes were dry and clean! Rafia had washed them. The smell of curry and smoke was gone. It was like lake water and soap-nuts now.

"Rafia, tell me! Why . . . ?"

"Sshh, Hafiz! Listen while you dress! And don't hurry so; you will break the strings!"

First there were the cotton pajamas, wide-legged, tight at the ankle, gathered in around his waist with a drawstring. Over the trousers was a little cotton shirt, with the tail hanging out. Then a wool coat, put on over his head, and another wool coat with wide sleeves, open all the way down the front. Rafia said he could try wearing just two coats now. "But," she added severely, "if you are cold you are to say it. Mind now!"

The little boy nodded, but he was more interested in the outside affair. He was dressed, all but his shoes. Shoes? He had forgot. They were in the lake.

Rafia said, "Wait until the farmer goes away. Abdullah will get your shoes."

So Hafiz had to sit down in the doorway with Rafia and look outside. Abdullah and his father and mother stood together in the bow of the boat. The farmer and his coolie sat in a *shikara* pulled alongside. The man was so angry he couldn't sit in his place. Once he almost fell in the water. Rafia had to put her hand over Hafiz' mouth quickly to stop the sound of his delighted chuckle.

The coolie was having no part in the talk. He had to hold the boat steady with a paddle. It was not easy, because the farmer moved about so much.

No one else laughed, only Hafiz. They were talking about him, he discovered. The farmer was demanding money for helping him out of the water!

"But I have no money!" the father insisted. "This is the end of the winter and the new season is not yet begun. How could I have any money left? I, a man with a family!"

"That one has!" said the farmer, pointing to

Abdullah.

The big boy shook his head.

"But I saw you give money to the baby," the farmer insisted stubbornly.

"And I am no baby," said Hafiz to Rafia under his breath.

"Ssh, Hafiz!" said Rafia for the dozenth time. "Listen to the talk!"

"You pay the child and you cannot pay me!" The farmer would not give up.

"Two coppers!" said Abdullah. "How much do you want?"

"One rupee!" said the farmer, hopefully.

Abdullah laughed. "So then, saving a child is worth one rupee. What is your price for saving a man?"

"A man could save himself!"

From his place in the doorway, Hafiz could see the farmer's scornful expression.

"And what makes you think the child could

not save himself? Or that the girl here might not have found a way?"

"The girl asked me to help."

The father said, "Let be, son, this is going far enough!"

At that moment, the farmer started to stand up and his boat tilted. The coolie grabbed his shirt to pull him down again, and lost his paddle. He leaned out to get that, but had to let go of the farmer. Before they knew it, both men were struggling in the water. Hafiz' family watched them calmly. The jerky clash of the silver bracelets was still as the mother stood quietly by her tall son. The men would not be hurt.

"Perhaps a dip in the lake will cool his hot blood," Abdullah muttered.

Hafiz would not stay with Rafia any longer. He got up and rushed out to see the fun more easily. The smooth boards felt hot to his bare feet and he felt thin in only two coats. It was a nice feeling. He went to his mother and reached for her hand.

The father took a boat hook from its ledge and helped put the *shikara* right side up. The farmer and his coolie climbed back in it, silently. The useful boat hook rescued the paddle too, which the coolie accepted with a quick salaam.

When they were settled, the farmer shook his fist at them all.

"You shall not stay at this tie-up this season!" he threatened. "I will see to it. Tomorrow!"

"What can you do?" Hafiz' father asked the question mildly. He smiled, which did not help the farmer's temper. "You do not own this land. You only rent your field. And I paid my renting fee today. Here is my paper!" The big, bearded man drew out of his clothing an envelope with the State seal on it in a big red splash.

The farmer motioned to the coolie that they would go. "You will see," he said, darkly. "I have ways!"

No one paid any attention to that. Hafiz tugged at his mother's hand. She looked down at him, smiling. The bracelets chimed again when she patted his head.

"A very small cause for all that trouble," she said fondly.

"Were there any sweets at the name day, my mother? Did they send me some? That baby, that wood-carver baby, how has he got my name?"

"Sweets? Here are the sweets they sent. The name? Thy father will tell thee at the time of the evening star!"

5

A PROMISE IS MADE

HAFIZ CARRIED HIS SWEETS TO THE WILLOW root. They were in a small basket made by pinning green leaves together with bits of their own stems. There were two squares of cooked sugar, cocoanut, and milk; there was a large, cream-colored ball that had white crumbly cheese inside; and there were two delicate criss-crossed rings that would be full of syrup when he ate them.

He looked at his riches and poked the top ones aside to see the next layer. Plump walnut meats and raisins! It must have been a very good party indeed. He must remember to ask if they had had a party on his name day.

Which sweet should he eat first? He chose a walnut meat and half of one of the cocoanut squares. The big sticky thing was his favorite. He would save that for the last.

The sun, shining through the new willow leaves, patched his coat with dark designs. But the ground was cold and he drew his bare feet up and tucked them in with the hem of his coat. Too late he realized it would be dirty when he got up. What would Rafia say?

Below him, in the pool, protected by the willow root, the little boats were still tied as he had left them the night before. They had been sheltered from the storm, and he could see no damage. There had not yet been time to give the soldier his ride. But he remembered the two coppers and what he ought to do with them. He got up and went back to the *doonga*. The basket of sweets was turned over to Rafia. She opened the lid of the stores box and set it inside. She did not see the dirt on his coat.

Hafiz went over to the crack and picked up the two coppers. He carried them, one in each hand, to the willow root. He knelt down, laid the money in the path, and untied the *shikara*. He lifted it out of the water. The bottom was wet so he dried it with the wide sleeve of his coat. Again, and too late, he remembered the lake was full of water plants. Their thick green coloring in still pools like this one would come off. He looked at his sleeve. There, as if it had been painted on, was a dull green streak across the inner side of his left sleeve. Poor Rafia!

Carefully he tugged at the little seat, after folding the small curtains up on top. The padded inch of wood came out of the grooves that grandfather had made, and stayed in his hand. The place beneath was clean and dry. Grand-

father had made a false bottom for the boat
and had told him the space between would hold
any small thing he wanted to put there. Nothing
had been said about money, but his money
would fit in.

"Fees!" said Hafiz, softly. "School fees!"
Perhaps some day, if he collected many coppers,
he could go to school.

The little *shikara* had just been returned to
the water when he heard Abdullah calling him.
It sounded far away. Where could Abdullah be?

Hafiz shouted in answer and ran along the
path and up the plank to the *doonga*. Abdullah
was out in the channel in the *shikara*.

"Ho, there, sailor! Show me where you fell
in so I can search for the little shoes!"

"Let me come, too, Abdullah! I will help.
And I will sit still."

Abdullah started paddling and brought the
shikara alongside. He held it steady with one

hand and helped Hafiz in with the other. Hafiz showed him where to look, in the clear water at the stern. Abdullah decided they needed more help, so he paddled back once again and hailed Rafia. If she would come, she could scull while Abdullah used the boat hook.

Rafia did not want to come. There was supper to be thought of and she and her mother had not finished their rice-husking. It had been a topsy-turvy day. There was a friendly argument. Finally Rafia got in and sat down. With a quick, continuous sweep of her arms she had picked up the paddle, settled her thin woolen scarf more securely on her hair, and was ready.

Abdullah took the boat hook and stood up in the bow. He was showing off, but it was fun. Hafiz sat on the seat in the middle and held on with both hands.

When Abdullah signaled, Rafia banked her paddle and swung the boat round a little. It stopped with a grand swish of water. Abdullah looked over the side. He thrust the boat hook down and brought up a water plant, root and all. They laughed and Abdullah tried again.

Hafiz looked cautiously over the side. He could see dozens of wee fish darting about, in and out of the water plants. And there were his shoes! The sun slanted down through the green growth in just the right way to let him see them. One was half under the plants, but the other was upside down on a patch of light sand. He called to Abdullah excitedly and the big boy tried again.

"My shoes! Abdullah, there they are!" Hafiz forgot to hold on to the seat, and clapped his hands. "Get them quickly, my brother!"

Abdullah sent the boat hook down again and seemed to be working very carefully over the spot where the shoes were. This time he brought up a rusty tin can. It was very disap-

pointing. Could Abdullah not see the shoes? Hafiz tried again.

He called to Abdullah to come to the middle of the boat and sit in his place, so he could see better. The little boy moved carefully as they changed positions. Falling in the lake once in a day was enough.

"Now, Hafiz! Ready! Show me the place!"

Hafiz leaned against Abdullah's knee and his voice rose shrilly.

"There!" said Hafiz, pointing almost straight down. Three times he said, "There!" and every time Abdullah looked the wrong way.

Hafiz turned round to Rafia for help. She was stuffing her scarf in her mouth to keep from laughing. Then he knew! Abdullah had already seen the shoes. He was just having fun.

"You are making a joke!" Hafiz accused them both.

"All right, sailor! We shall get the shoes now.

Then do I get a sweet?"

"Everybody wants pay for things!" said Hafiz. "But . . . you may have all my sweets, Abdullah . . . well, all but the big round one."

"You do not get one sweet, Abdullah!" declared Rafia. "You know the mother brought them for Hafiz. It is a present from Hafiz to Hafiz," she teased.

But Hafiz would not have it that way. "My mother brought it for me," he said, firmly.

Even after Abdullah really set to work to get the shoes out of the water it was not easy. The boat hook caught on the water plants and so did the shoes. Twice he had the second shoe almost in the boat and it fell back again. The third time he caught it by the tip and set it on the seat in the bow, by its mate. So they were out of the water again, two little shoes of Kashmir leather, with curling tips and no heels.

A PROMISE IS MADE

The leather was thoroughly soaked. Rafia took the shoes to the cooking place and wiped them dry with an old cloth. She pressed out all of the water possible and smeared them with some cooking oil. The shoes stood all night above the warm ashes, but when Hafiz tried to put them on next day, they were stiff and he couldn't get his feet in comfortably.

Rafia took them in her hand and rubbed and rubbed with the oil. "Play in your bare feet to-day," she urged. "Perhaps tonight they will be soft."

At night they were still too small. They hurt his toes. The leather had drawn up hopelessly. The soles were peeling off in shreds and the stitching was broken. There were wide holes between the sole and the top of each shoe.

The father sat in the corner enjoying his after-supper smoke. His water-pipe stood in front of him on the floor. He watched Hafiz struggle with the shoes.

Presently Hafiz laid the shoes down and looked at the water-pipe. When the smoker drew the smoke up through the long slanting pipe stem, the water below the coals made a "hubble, bubble" sound. Smoke meant sound and smell together, therefore, to Hafiz. He never grew tired of the fascinating ritual, from the preparation of the pipe to the last faint gurgle of the water. He had seen it often, but each time it was new again.

At length the big man pushed the pipe stem away and held out his hand for the shoes. He saw all the things that were wrong. He smiled at Hafiz.

"So!" said he. "A man must have shoes! If the Sahib pays his rent in advance when he comes, we will go to the street of the leather workers. You and I together! We will find you a pair of shoes!"

6

ABDULLAH READS A LETTER

IT WAS MORE THAN TWO WEEKS BEFORE
another letter came from the Sahib. It had gone
first to the wood-carver's house. There, Sayyad
Khan, owner of the largest shop at Third
Bridge, had seen it, and had offered to leave it

on his way to the Gate.

Hafiz was at the willow root when he saw Sayyad Khan's boat pulling alongside in mid-morning. He edged along the path as far as the plank to see better. His mother left the rice-husking and went in to the cooking place to prepare the pipe. This important visitor must be invited to take a puff or two.

Sayyad Khan stayed in his boat, however, and refused the friendly gesture. He had his own pipe, he said. He offered the letter to the father, who took it and handed it to his elder son. Abdullah opened the envelope slowly and read, while the others watched. He mumbled the English words to himself. Then he waited, but Sayyad Khan did not go. Instead, the merchant leaned forward and asked, "Are you not going to share your news?"

He leaned back comfortably. He had come in his shop boat but there was a canopy over his head and fat cushions were piled on the rich rug spread on the bottom of his boat. Behind him was a heap of carved wood and rolls of rugs for sale.

Hafiz crept up behind Abdullah to listen. Abdullah cleared his throat importantly, and spat over the side. He held up the letter and looked only at his father.

"The Sahib says here, my father, that he wishes all of us well. He asks Allah's favor on all in this household."

The father bowed, as if thanking the Sahib in person.

"Furthermore," Abdullah went on, a little louder, "he hopes that that rascal, Sayyad Khan, remembers the torn rug he showed last summer and that he will be the first to call upon him, bringing a good one."

Everybody laughed, though a little uncertainly; Sayyad Khan too, though he did not look pleased. They knew that was not in the letter. Abdullah was only having fun. But it was true that Sayyad Khan had tried to sell the Sahib a bad rug.

Their father swung his pipe stem aside. "Get on with it, son! Do not keep Sayyad Khan waiting!"

Hafiz did not understand why his father did not like the fun, but he thought the man should have gone away then. This was their own family letter.

Sayyad Khan did not intend to be cheated of the first summer news, however. He would use it to good purpose later, Hafiz knew. When he played in the shavings at the wood-carver's he heard many things. The workmen squatted before their low benches and gossiped about half the Valley while they chiseled and shaped and smoothed the lovely woods.

"The Sahib says," Abdullah started again in

a singsong tone, "that he is very pleased to be having our boat again." Sayyad Khan looked surprised. The father bowed once more, with an eye toward Sayyad Khan to see if he were impressed.

"Some day I shall be reading out English letters like this," Hafiz thought, "if I can go to school." It would feel very grand. He wished Abdullah would hurry. He wanted to know when the Sahib would come. How much longer might he have to wait for the new shoes?

"On this page," said Abdullah, turning the letter over, "the Sahib says he will come . . ." he hesitated and counted on his fingers . . . "one week from last Saturday."

He folded the letter and put it in his pocket. There was a little silence. Sayyad Khan waited, but there were no comments from the group. Hafiz knew that Abdullah had not read all of the letter.

Sayyad Khan cleared his throat. "Now that you are to have a tenant, I can expect a payment?" he inquired smoothly. His dark eyes glittered.

Abdullah shifted his feet. He looked uneasy. Hafiz saw his father's impatient gesture before he tucked his hands out of sight, beneath his loose coat sleeves.

"I have no money now, Sayyad Khan. I have told you that! When the Sahib pays, I will pay." The father spoke very quietly.

Sayyad Khan did not yet know that tone as the family did. The big man was angry. He had not liked Abdullah's fun with the letter. And he did not care to discuss money when the whole family was present.

So the father owed Sayyad Khan money! He was the most feared and therefore the most hated moneylender in the Valley. Hafiz had heard the talk in the bazaar. Why had the father done this? What was the money for? Their rice? They had not bought anything else all winter. This was the reason there had been no money for shoes.

Sayyad Khan was speaking again. "Your farmer neighbor tells me a different story," he said, silkily, meanly. "He says you have money."

There was another small silence. "The farmer . . ." began Abdullah, but the father held up his hand, and Abdullah was still again.

"I have an unrented boat, much better than yours! Perhaps the Sahib might be persuaded to rent it instead." Sayyad Khan smiled and stroked his beard. "I could get this tie-up, too, if he likes it."

Hafiz heard Abdullah draw in an angry breath. "But we have . . ." he began, in spite of the father's warning.

It was Sayyad Khan who interrupted him

73

this time. "Yes, I know," he said mockingly, "you have a renting paper, with a seal. But there are ways . . . yes, there are ways!" He settled himself more comfortably on his cushions and smiled again, provokingly, at his little audience.

"How shall you profit if I have no tenant?" the father inquired. "Besides," he added proudly, "I have the Sahib's letter that he will rent my boat. If you believe the gossip of coolies and farmers more than my saying, which is the word of a true Moslem, then may you have a season of empty boats!"

The visitor motioned to his paddlers to push off and the father was allowed the last word.

"You will have your money. I have said it!"

Hafiz was troubled. Sayyad Khan was a powerful merchant. If he took all their money for the debt, whatever it was for, would there be any left to buy shoes?

74

ABDULLAH READS A LETTER

Abdullah did not bring the letter out again until Sayyad Khan was away, beyond the bend in the channel.

"Now, my father," said he, "I shall read all of the letter. It has been long on the way. The Sahib will be at the Dal Gate the day after to-morrow!"

"So soon!" thought Hafiz. "At the Gate, where the lake joins the river! Only a little way from this boat! The day after tomorrow!" Abdullah made everything sound all right again. He could almost feel the new shoes on his feet. Then he remembered Sayyad Khan and felt more barefoot than before.

Abdullah frowned his way through the letter from the beginning, until he found the place he was looking for.

"Ah! Here it is! The Sahib says it might be a good idea to have the houseboat cleaned well, before he comes!"

The father said nothing, but their mother was pleased, very pleased. "Said I not so?" she demanded. "This is a very smart Sahib. But now you have only one day to do the work of many. If Hafiz were a man, he could help you." She glanced round at her menfolk. "You will need help!" she added.

Rafia nodded her head in agreement. The women were enjoying this very much.

Hafiz said, "But I can help. My father called me a man!"

His mother's bracelets jingled as she drew him closer to her. "What can you do?" she asked.

"I can help," the little boy insisted, at the same time pulling away from the circle of her arm. It was the first time he had ever done that. But men were not treated so. He would be obliged to help tomorrow and that was man's work.

There was more of the letter. The Sahib had used much ink. He wanted them to meet him at the Gate with the *shikara*.

In two more days the Sahib would come! There was work to do, much work. Hafiz wondered if he should clean the little boats, too. There might not be time if he were helping his father in the big one. Why did they not start work now, at once?

While he had been daydreaming, his mother was asking the same question. All of her bracelets were chiming. Her hands were not still a minute as she talked, and she was talking very fast. Here was a day made for work, a beautiful clear day, and a job of work to do. Why not begin? But she could stir neither Abdullah nor his father. They said there would be plenty of time tomorrow.

The discussion went on and on between Abdullah and the mother. He assured her, over and over again, that everything would be all right.

The father was still. He had turned again to his pipe but he was not drinking the smoke. He was looking far away to the mountains beyond the marsh, but not seeing them. For the first time a debt had been mentioned aloud and Say-yad Khan's threats had power. Hafiz went over to his father and sat down quietly. After a while the women went back to their neglected rice-husking. Abdullah got into the *shikara* and went away, without telling anyone where he was going.

7

HAFIZ HELPS

HAFIZ WOKE NEXT MORNING WITH THAT nice feeling which always comes when something special is about to happen. Not that he was sure how special housecleaning could be. He had never helped before.

"That is because I was a baby," he thought.

"Now that my father has called me a man, I can help!"

He was the first one ready to start the day. Abdullah was in no hurry. His father sat longer than usual over his pipe. The eager little boy thought much time was being wasted. He wanted to skip teeth, but Rafia insisted. He faced her with his hands behind his back and shook his head.

"But you want to be a strong man, don't you?" she pleaded.

"My father says I am a man now, Rafia!" he reminded her. He was very dignified. It was important to make everything clear. "I do not see my father do his teeth every morning."

Rafia shrugged her shoulders. "That does not mean he does not do them."

"Did he do teeth every morning when he was a little boy?"

"We were not here then, so how can I say?"

Hafiz thought about it for a moment.

Rafia said, "You do not want teeth like Sayyad Khan's when you are old."

Hafiz remembered Sayyad Khan's yellow stumps. Perhaps it might be as well to take the time this morning, as usual. Having nice white teeth might help him get into the school. Rafia would not know about such things. Girls did not go to school.

While chewing the willow brush Hafiz saw Abdullah come out. The big brother looked up at the clear sky and frowned. The day was fair. It was plain to Hafiz that Abdullah had hoped for rain. That was strange. Why should he want to miss the fun of cleaning the houseboat? Hafiz began to doubt. Maybe helping wasn't going to be something special, after all. Abdullah liked fun, always.

When their father finished his pipe and said, "Come, son!" Abdullah followed silently along the runway, to the front door of the house-boat.

Hafiz had almost finished his teeth when there came a sound of banging and pounding. After that, Rafia could not hold him. He had flatly refused breakfast earlier. He was not hungry! And now he had to see what was making that noise.

The houseboat faced the morning sun. Above its front door a carved bird, looking very much like a big fat goose, had been painted blue. Over its head the boat's name, *Blue Heron*, was cut into the soft pine wood.

The door was in two parts, joining in the middle. A hasp with a padlock stuck through the staple held the halves together.

Abdullah was making the noise. He stood at the door, pounding with his fist and tugging at the lock.

"Why are you doing that, Abdullah? Why

doesn't the door open? I want to go inside. I can help! I brushed my teeth!"

Hafiz stopped for breath and Abdullah stopped working at the door. He grinned at the earnest, solemn little face.

"You really want to help, don't you, Small One?"

Hafiz nodded, looking very puzzled.

"Well then, right now you can help most by just keeping still! The key is stuck in the lock. It will not turn." Abdullah went on pounding at it and trying to move the key.

Hafiz sat down on the first step of the narrow stairway leading to the little deck on the roof of the boat. He could hear his father tramping about up there. He heard a clicking and a snipping sound, too.

Holding tight to the shaky handrail with one hand, while the other held up his coat, Hafiz climbed the steps. When his eyes were on a level with the deck, he stopped. His father was cutting away some of the willow branches which hung like a green curtain on the land side.

The whole world looked different up here. The mountains were very blue this morning and there were soft fat clouds sailing along below their tops. One cloud was pink from the morning sun. Looking below, Hafiz could see the mountains and the clouds again in the lake water, but they were upside down.

It would be nice, he thought, to go all the way up the steps and talk to his father. He would enjoy looking at the clouds in the lake, too. But most of all he wanted to watch Abdullah. He backed down again.

The door was still shut. Abdullah kicked it. He looked cross. Suddenly Hafiz did not like sitting on the steps any longer. He got up and crossed the plank to the path.

Back in the *doonga* Rafia was finishing the morning bread. She did not hear Hafiz coming because he did not have shoes.

"Rafia!" he began, importantly.

Rafia jumped when she felt his hand on her shoulder. She dropped a piece of dough on the red coals. There was a dreadful smell. She picked it up with the tongs and tossed it through the door into the lake.

Hafiz said her name again. "Rafia, I must have the bread tongs!" he announced. He was only a little higher than her head when she leaned toward the fire, but it made him feel very tall, standing there beside her in his long coat.

"And what will you do with the bread tongs, my boatman? Has thy fleet sunk to the bottom of the pool at the willow root? Have you to fish out the little boats?"

"Rafia, you mustn't make jokes. I am very

busy. I am helping. We need the tongs!"

"Oh, we do, do we?" Rafia mocked, laughing. She tried to hold him close to her, but he drew away, snatched the tongs and ran, chuckling. He expected her to follow him, but she did not.

At the door of the *Blue Heron,* Hafiz found his father and Abdullah both working at the lock. Hafiz offered the tongs. Abdullah got the idea at once.

"Ha, Hafiz, the very thing! Why did I not think of it?"

Abdullah held the key tightly with the tongs, keeping the lock firm with his other hand. He gave the key a twist. The rust inside gritted slowly out of the way. The lock fell open. Abdullah took it out of the staple and laid it on the step where Hafiz had been sitting. He handed the tongs back to Hafiz.

"There, Small One, that was fine help. Take

these back to Rafia now. We do not want her to come looking for them."

Hafiz said nothing. He took the tongs and turned away. If he returned them to Rafia now, he would miss going into the boat with Abdullah. His feet went slower and slower. He had got as far as the willow root. He stopped. Suddenly he laid the tongs down in the path and scurried back aboard the *Blue Heron*.

So, after all, the little boy was at the elder one's heels when the door was at last opened on creaking hinges. Abdullah swung the halves back and forth. The hinges still made a dreadful noise. "Oil!" he exclaimed, and sighed.

The place did not smell like any Hafiz knew. The mat house he lived in smelled of the dried herbs in the rafters and lake winds and cooking smoke. He could not name the parts of this mixture. Abdullah could have told him it was pine wood and dusty floor matting, kerosene

87

lamps and moldy books. There was a tumbled row of old books in one of the shelves opposite the door.

Abdullah hurried to open the windows. They slid on little metal runners into the wall. Hafiz watched with big eyes. He had never been inside this boat. On the lake side only the glass windows were pushed back. The window openings were still covered by wire netting. On the land side Abdullah ran the wire windows into the wall, too.

Hafiz looked around. The first room they had entered seemed very small. But it was as wide as the boat itself. It had wooden walls, like the outside of the boat. Every knothole in the pine paneling showed. But it felt smooth, like Rafia's hair after it had been freshly oiled and braided.

The father stood outside in the path. He called to Abdullah to hand him the furniture through the windows.

"What shall I do, Abdullah?" their small helper demanded.

"Just be patient, Small One!"

Hafiz knew what that meant. Abdullah did not like what he himself was doing. How could he have ideas for anyone else? Hafiz did not want to be patient. That was just sitting still. Perhaps he ought to take the tongs back to Rafia. He stood in the doorway, trying to decide.

Abdullah lifted the chairs through the window first. There were three of them, of willow, made in the Valley. In the corner was a square table. It had a thick felt cover which hung almost to the floor. Abdullah twitched the cover off and bundled the wadded-up folds into Hafiz' arms.

"Here, Hafiz," he said, "can you carry this outdoors? It will be helping."

There was too much of the cover for Hafiz to hold easily. One corner hung down. He could not see where he was going. He tripped on the corner and fell full length on the floor. He bit his tongue and cut his lip against a sharp tooth when he fell. He roared.

Abdullah came and separated boy from cover. He threw the cloth after the chairs before he examined Hafiz' bumps. The little boy sat on the floor, crying. His lip was swelling. He stuck his tongue out to see how the place felt. Abdullah leaned over him and helped him up.

"Now, now, be a good boatman!" he soothed. He rubbed Hafiz' head. "That was not a bad tumble. You have had harder ones. Look! I will put you up high, where you can see everything and not fall."

Hafiz found himself on the top bookshelf. There was room for him to sit because there were no books up here and the niche which held the shelves was arched at the top. When the father called Abdullah outside, Hafiz was left alone.

Outdoors, the springtime world was soft gold in the sunlight. The sounds of busy ducks, feeding, and the well-song from the field came in the open window. Hafiz could not see anything. He did not like that place and wished he could get down. He stuck out one foot, trying to reach down to the next shelf. His foot struck a book and the book went plop on the floor. It hit another book on the way down and the whole row tumbled after it. Then Hafiz leaned out too far to see what was happening and he, too, fell right on top of the heap of books. He was too surprised to cry out.

Abdullah and his father both came when they heard the books falling. They looked at Hafiz and then at each other. All three laughed.

Hafiz chuckled more than the others. At least he had got down from the shelf. Abdullah pulled him up and put a book under each arm.

"Now then, boatman, carry the books outdoors! That will really help us!"

They went back to the dining room. Loud noises there meant that the table and chairs were going out through the window, too.

Hafiz sat down on the floor again, to look at the books. These were not nice ones like Abdullah's school books. They had no pictures. And they were very dusty. He might as well carry them out. Abdullah had said it would be helping. So he picked them up, two at a time, one under each arm, and marched out over the plank to the chairs on the runway. He piled the books in the chairs. The bread tongs were forgotten.

On the last trip he looked up at the shelf where he had sat. That was the first time he saw himself in a real mirror. He did not know what that shiny place could be, beside the book-shelves.

There was a boy coming toward him. That other boy was dressed in a long coat, too, and his face was very dirty. His lip was swollen and he had been crying. Why, it was another Hafiz! Every time he rubbed his hands on his coat that boy did. When he walked up to the glass and flattened his nose against it, the other Hafiz met him there.

Abdullah found him like that, face pressed against the mirror.

"So," said Abdullah, "you have found that other Small One!" He was smiling. "You will have to tell him good-by now. I am come to take up the rugs."

Hafiz stood on a rug and Abdullah pulled. He rode only a little way. Then Abdullah gave the rug a big tug, and down went Hafiz again.

He had expected it, however, and was ready for another. But before he could stand up, Abdullah rolled him off the rug onto the matting underneath. Whoosh! The rugs went out the window in a long roll.

The matting, with Hafiz in the middle, and only his head and feet sticking out, went next. His father seemed very surprised when that wriggling roll appeared. He lifted Hafiz out of the matting and set him gently in the path. Hafiz' mouth was full of dust and he was coughing and sneezing.

"Have you given your soldier a ride today? Have you looked well to the little boats?" asked the father.

"No, but they are all right," Hafiz insisted. He sneezed again. "I want to help you now."

Abdullah put his head through the window just then. "Shall I take up the floor panel, my father?" he asked.

The big man stood quietly a moment, smoothing his beard. There were bits of willow leaf and matting shreds caught in it. "Wait!" he said. He leaned from the runway to look inside the houseboat. Hafiz clamored to see, too. His father lifted him in his strong arms back through the window.

"Here I am again, Abdullah! See me?"

Abdullah took the little boy out of his father's arms and pretended to push him back out again, the way he had come. Hafiz squirmed and Abdullah set him down.

He was listening to his father who was still in the window, thinking out loud. There was thick dust in little ridges on the floor, making a pattern where the matting had been. It looked very dirty. The father shook his head doubtfully.

"The women said it should be made clean," he remarked. "And we have only one day. But

. . . yes . . . I think we ought to look at that floor beneath a floor."

He stepped over the window sill and stood with the two boys in the little living room of the *Blue Heron*. Hafiz could feel his heart thumping as it always did when there was something special going on.

Abdullah leaned down and tugged at the heavy iron ring sunk in the middle of the floor. He pulled. The whole center section of the floor moved. His father helped and they lifted it out. It was set against the outside wall by the windows.

The father breathed deeply in his beard. "Now we shall see what we shall see. It has been long and long since this floor was opened."

Hafiz crowded close to his father and held his hand. He did not want to fall down into that hole in the floor. Did all boats have floors upon floors like this one? Was that why his

96

shikara had been made with two floors? Was there a place like this beneath the floor in the *doonga?* He did not ask his questions now. He did not want to talk. There was too much to see.

8

MORE LOST THINGS APPEAR

THE SPACE BENEATH THE FLOOR WAS NOT very deep. It was really the curved bottom of the boat they were looking at. Here and there, on the slanting sides, were wet patches where the water had seeped in from the lake.

It was a place to delight any boy. All the

odds and ends of boat gear for which there was no other place had been put beneath the floor. Some of it was tucked in on the crossbeams to be safe from dampness. On top of the heap in the middle was a roll of faded green canvas.

"There is the awning for the deck!" exclaimed the father. "I did not rig it last summer. The Sahib did not ask for it. Hand it up, boy!"

Abdullah sat with his feet down in the hole. He tugged and laid the heavy canvas on the floor beside him. The father turned it over with his foot. It had a damp smell, Hafiz decided. The father said, "It will be well to use it this year. An improvement will add to the rent!"

His elder son laughed. Abdullah was enjoying this search into family treasures more than pushing tables and chairs out of windows. He held up a lantern which had no chimney.

"That is the lantern the hospital sent when Hafiz was born. We forgot to take it back. . . . But they never asked for it! Ah! Well!" The father looked down at Hafiz.

"It brought us luck to have another man in the family. We like to keep lucky things!"

Hafiz wriggled like a puppy that has had its head patted. He felt good all over. He forgot his bumps and cut lip. Helping was fun, after all. He would like to have that lantern for his own. He could use it when he went out to look at the little boats at night. If they got it when he was born, was it not really his? A sort of name day gift!

He came out of that daydream to hear what Abdullah was saying. "Shall I take out anything more?"

"Yes," said the father, "let us have a good look. I, myself, have forgotten much that is here."

The canvas had covered a folding wooden table. Abdullah handed it out. The father opened the leaves and set it up. One hinge was broken. The big man chuckled.

"This is the table I rented from the Agency. They made me buy it when the first tenants that year took it to camp. . . . They were gone a long time." He seemed to be remembering out loud, more than he was talking to his sons. "I said they would bring it back, but the Agency wouldn't believe me. They did bring it back. But my money was spent. Now we have a good table."

The table folded up and fell, with a loud bang. Dust rose in clouds. Hafiz held his nose. His father set the table on top of the canvas beside the opening in the floor.

"Ai hai!" he exclaimed. "It is not so good after all. Well . . . a day will come, some other day, when we can take it to Third Bridge.

Perhaps they will have another hinge . . ."

His voice trailed off uncertainly as he returned to the present business. Abdullah had the shaft of a broken paddle and was poking about with it. He handed up an extra board for a landing plank, two folding chairs with slats falling out, and a large white china soup dish with a handle missing. Underneath the chairs he found a pasteboard box half full of white wax candles. They had been chewed by mice. A coil of rope and two oil lamp bases were off at one side.

"I thought we had some extra rope," said the father. "We will take that to the *doonga*. Leave the lamps. There will be the light-without-oil at this place when the Sahib comes."

The rope was piled with the table and the canvas, and the other things were put back in the hole. Abdullah was just ready to fit the floor panel in place again when the boat moved suddenly. Light streamed in from an empty knothole high on the living room wall. It shone down into the hole and for a second there was a glimpse of color, lovely bright color, to a little boy's eyes.

"Wait, Abdullah!" Hafiz begged. "Look! What is it? I saw something!"

At first Abdullah could not see anything unusual. Hafiz would not give up. He leaned way over and pointed into a corner where the crossbeam joined the side of the boat.

Abdullah looked again. He reached in and brought out something in his closed fist. He offered it to Hafiz, who put his two hands together to receive the surprise. The little boy was truly surprised, for it was not a thing he had ever seen. It was round and red and looked a bit like a smaller red clay water jar.

"A ball!" Abdullah exclaimed. "How did it get down there?"

It hit Hafiz' hands, then bounced softly against his face. He drew back, his eyes blinking, and the ball fell on his lap and rolled back into the hole. All three of them knelt on the floor and peered over the edge. There it was, between the lamp bases! This time the father got it out. Hafiz took it carefully. What a strange, soft thing it was!

While he sat there, turning the ball over and over, feeling it and wondering about it, his father and Abdullah were wondering, too. They looked at each other, silently asking again where the ball could have come from. None of their former tenants had had children. This rubber would still bounce, therefore it was not very old. They gave it up presently, agreeing as silently as they had wondered that sitting there would not give them the answer.

Abdullah leaned over and took the ball. He showed Hafiz how to make it bounce.

"See, Small One! This is like the big balls the boys use on the playing fields at school. You know volley ball? You know hockey? I have told you!"

A grin of pleased understanding spread over Hafiz' face. He saw now what this new play-thing might be like. If they meant him to have it. He held the ball up. "Is it for taking out-doors?"

His father answered. "Yes, go and play now! You have worked enough for one day. Play with the ball and the little boats and forget your bumps."

Hafiz was glad to be through with helping for a while. The bread tongs were in the path where he had left them. That made him think of food. It was midday by the sun, and he was hungry.

Rafia was sitting in the bow of the *doonga*, pulling dried peppers off a string. He gave her the tongs and asked for his basket of sweets. When she brought it, she offered him a piece of leftover bread. He chose the raisins from the basket, and sat down by Rafia to eat. The bread was cold and tough but he chewed it patiently.

It was beautiful in the sun. Across the channel the marsh grasses were showing new green among the tufts of last year's dead roots. A marsh hen was slowly poking in and out, hunting a place for a nest, no doubt. Her black feathers shaded to purple and green around her neck. Off to the north the white peaks glittered in the high sunlight.

From far away, above Gagribal, came the sound of the coolies' chant, rising and falling, falling and rising. They must be moving something heavy along the lake road.

"I like this place," said Hafiz. "Aren't you glad the Sahib likes it, too?"

"Yes, Hafiz," Rafia agreed. "It is a good

place. What is that in thy hand?"

"Bread," Hafiz chuckled, "and bread in my mouth, too!" He held out the ball. "And in this hand, Rafia, is a ball, found under the floor this morning." He bounced it in time to the chant, still clearly rising and falling on the upper lake.

Rafia looked at the ball, but she did not offer to touch it. She was more interested in the housecleaning.

"Playing with the things under the floor!" she teased. "Is that all the three of you did in one morning? Will the Sahib be able to get in the place when he comes?"

Hafiz assured her stoutly that they had all worked. "I carried books and I fell down, and Abdullah rolled me in the matting and I sneezed."

"You look like all of that," Rafia agreed again.

The little meal was almost finished when

there was a hail from the lake. A boat was bringing the water man. He had come to help wash the floors of the houseboat. He stood up and hoisted his goatskin to his hip. It was full and very heavy, so that he leaned over to walk and used a short stick. Hafiz ran along the path after him to watch.

All the furniture from the *Blue Heron* was out on the runway. The sweeper had come, too. He had cleaned the rugs and the matting and now he was inside, making noise and sending drifts of dust out through the windows into the bright spring air. He used a stout twig broom. The water man let little spurts of water out of the goatskin onto the floor by releasing the pressure of his thumb at the neck.

The sweeper swished it about until each floor was clean. Both men were barefooted. Their shoes were waiting outside in the path, so they would not get wet.

MORE LOST THINGS APPEAR

When the floors were clean and the men had gone away, Rafia brought her father's pipe and he sat down in the path for a smoke. Abdullah stretched out on the deck and went to sleep in the sun. It was very still, so that the water could be heard, dripping down from the sides of the boat into the lake. There was a good smell everywhere of wet pine, with the green odor of cut willow branches and the sweet smoke from the father's pipe. Hafiz thought again that it was a good place, a really wonderful one. But he did wish that Abdullah would wake up and play ball with him.

Everything had to be put back in the *Blue Heron* when the floors were dry. Hafiz wandered in and out and got in the way again. He went into the little galley in the middle of the boat, where Abdullah would later bring the Sahib's food. It had its own door and plank from the path. Hafiz sat down in the doorway and rolled the ball down the plank. He tried imagining what it would be like to have a boat like this, only a great deal smaller, that he could live in all by himself. It would be great fun.

The evening gun had boomed from the Fort before all was in order. Hafiz carried the books back in. Now, standing upside down and some with backs to the wall, they waited on their shelf for the guest to come. He had been to school surely, Hafiz thought, and he could read. Hafiz stood in the door and looked at the untidy row with great pride. He had been called a man that day, and he had helped.

When everything was neat, Abdullah locked all the doors from the inside, except the front one. He shooed Hafiz out ahead of him, and fastened the padlock in the staple. They stood for a moment looking up the lake. The light on the mountains was blue now, and very clear. It would be a fair day tomorrow.

Hafiz stopped at the willow root to see if the little boats were all right. They had not been out all day. He saw Abdullah take the *shikara* and start in the direction of the wood-carver's. He was probably going to get the bazaar news and see if there were any more letters. For a second the little boy thought of running after him. But no, he must see to the little boats.

They had all been out for a sail, and were re-tied to the root before Rafia called. He stopped only to push his long stick into the ground against the tree and to pick up the ball. He still did not know how to play with it very well. He was afraid, too, that it would roll into the water.

It was growing dusk and he was glad to be called. He had done a man's work and felt like sitting in the corner with the others. They might let him stay up late tonight. He started to run in the path.

The rubbish from the cleaning, which had collected there, made the ground feel differently tonight. Rolls of fine fluff from the woolly rugs were caught in the wilting leaves from the tree trimming. The fine dust from the matting felt thick and soft. The dry twigs broken from the sweeper's broom tickled his feet.

Hafiz had almost reached the plank to the *doonga,* when one foot struck something hard which went spinning ahead. He thought it was a stone until it hit the plank and there was a ringing sound. He stooped and felt in the path where the plank rested on the ground. His hand closed on something round and hard and flat.

He rubbed it against his coat, adding another streak to the many already showing on the clean surface which the soap-nuts had made. It might be money! He thought it was. Wonderful! He hurried up the plank, and as he crossed to the door he saw the *shikara* coming back.

"Hurry, Abdullah!" he called. "Here is a thing! What is it? If I found it, is it mine? Is it money?"

They went in the door together, after Hafiz had impatiently waited for the *shikara* painter to be slipped through its ring at the bow of the *doonga*.

The firelight caught the silver sheen of a coin when Hafiz opened his hand.

"It is money, my boatman!" pronounced Abdullah. "You have found a rupee!"

Rafia delayed serving supper while the family asked many questions. A whole rupee! Where had he found it? Where had it come from? Who could have lost it? What should be done with it?

Abdullah and his father teased the little boy. Abdullah said, "Perhaps you should give it to the farmer for hauling you up out of the lake. He thinks he needs a rupee!"

And his father said, "That is more than one man's fair wage for a day's work, my son! Do you think it earned today?"

Hafiz took that seriously. He thought a minute. "I carried books," he argued gravely. "And I brought the bread tongs!" he added.

"So you did, boy, so you did!"

Then everybody laughed, and once more, too late, Hafiz knew they had only been having fun. But he did notice that his mother and Rafia did not have much to say about the wonderful find. Women were not supposed to know about money anyway. It was the men who bought the rice and cleaned boats and read letters!

Abdullah and his father decided that the coin must have fallen out of the chair cushions. Someone could have lost it from a pocket or a wallet. There was really no way, however, to find out whose the money might have been.

"Maybe it was for Sayyad Khan and it was lost in the chair, so he never got it," Hafiz suggested.

"Sayyad Khan gets everything that is his. He always sees to that," Abdullah declared darkly.

Finally the father said Hafiz should keep the money, partly because he had found it, but more because they would not be able to find the owner.

Hafiz rubbed the coin once more against his coat. Then he laid it on the floor in plain sight, while he ate his supper out of the bowl which Rafia filled for him.

9

HAFIZ NAMES HIS SHIKARA

IT WAS WARMER THAT NIGHT THAN IT HAD yet been. At bedtime Rafia did not pull all the mats down. Abdullah and his father had gone back to the houseboat but Hafiz was sent to his quilt. The dark did not come completely because there was a moon. It made a path across the water to the boat.

Before he lay down, Hafiz tilted the rupee in the crack by the soldier. The little guard had stood there stiffly many days and nights, waiting for the promised ride.

At first, everything was very still outside. It was so still that Hafiz could hear the clatter of crockery from the houseboat. Abdullah was there in the little pantry, washing all the dishes.

Rafia and her mother sat outside in the bow of the *doonga*. They were laughing and having fun. They had had fun all day. Abdullah and his father had not liked that laughter.

Only Hafiz had to lie on his bed. His quilt made him too warm. He threw part of it back, over his feet.

The frogs in the marshes began their croaking that night. Everything in the world was awake. It was the lovely moonlight. Hafiz sat up and looked about him. He could see the snow peaks, faintly, far away against the sky. There were little bright sparkles once in a while, where the moonlight and the frost up there came together.

When a tiny wind stirred the water, the boat shifted a bit. The path of light stretched all the way to Hafiz' feet. It reached the place in the crack where the little soldier stood. The polished coin at his side glittered.

Hafiz picked up the money and began playing with it. He lay down flat on his back and made a hill in the quilt with his knees. Down the hill and into the valleys he slid the silver coin, again and again.

In all his eight years Hafiz had never owned this much money. He felt very rich. The family had asked what he would buy with it. A rupee would buy many things. He could have a whole platoon of clay soldiers. He did not know how many baskets of sweets it would get for him. There was the toy houseboat, too, that he had been longing for. He could buy that, he knew, and still have half of his money left.

The coin coasted down the quilt hill once more and disappeared. Hafiz hunted, but it was gone. Was there a place where it might have slipped beneath the floor? Once more he wondered if there were a floor beneath the floor in this boat, too. He crawled all the way outside the quilt. He shook it. He heard a ringing sound then, but still could not see the rupee.

His mother called: "Lie down, my son! A full day is behind thee! Sleep now!"

Hafiz lay down quietly enough, until the women began talking again. He did want to find the coin. He felt with his hands on either side of the mat, up and down as far as he could stretch. There it was, at last. It had rolled over against the corner of the stores box. It lay flat on the floor.

His little fist closed on it. Then he bit the edge as they sometimes did in the bazaar. That was to see if it were good silver. How could they tell? This money had a horrible taste. He wished he had one of his sweets.

Tomorrow he would put the new coin away with the coppers in the little boat. He would not buy anything. Not at once. He did not know how much school fees were. But he would not spend any of this until he could find out.

The thought of the *shikara*, and what the sliding seat would hide for him, made him smile. What a beautiful little boat his *shikara* was! Grandfather had done his work well. And his new money was beautiful. Two lovely things together!

The moon had climbed higher. From the edge of the marsh, over the water, right up to

Hafiz' chin, there was now a wide road. It was the same color as his shining money.

He lay turning the coin and watching for the sparkle when it slanted the right way in the moonlight. Its shape, too, was like the moon's, he thought. Round, and the same color! There was a silver-colored moon up in the sky, and he had a little one in his hand.

Quite suddenly Hafiz knew another thing. He had found a name for the *shikara*. The *Silver Moon!* What a splendid name! And he had thought of it all by himself. Tomorrow he would ask Abdullah to put the new name on the *shikara,* just as the houseboat had its name above the door.

The *Silver Moon!* He repeated it softly, several times. Rafia came and asked if he had called. He said he wanted a drink of water. She brought him some and straightened his quilt. She lowered a mat to shut out the light.

After Rafia had gone, Hafiz turned on his side and once more laid the coin beside the little soldier. Tomorrow the soldier really should have his ride, in a boat with its own name.

Hafiz had forgotten the rubber ball. It lay all night in the runway where he had dropped it when he stooped to pick up the rupee.

10

THE NEW TENANT ARRIVES

THERE WERE DOZENS OF *SHIKARAS* MOORED
at different points in Dal Gate next morning
when Hafiz and Abdullah and their father
slowly paddled in. One place was left at the
foot of the steps leading up the lake bank to
the road.

A line of houseboats lay out in the stream.
A few of their owners were part of the noisy

crowd above on the bank. Sometimes people came without making arrangements for boats beforehand. A motor bus from the India plains was due any moment and private cars were already arriving.

A Kashmiri policeman stood on the steps, trying to keep them clear. Two treads at the bottom were badly broken and accidents would be easy. The water lapped noisily around the jagged wood.

On the left of the steps a row of taxi-boats looked very gay in the morning sun. Their bright curtains and fresh cushions made the dingy *shikaras* look much worse. Each had a gay new sign, too. All of the signs said they had spring seats.

Hafiz and Abdullah stayed in the boat while their father went up to the road to wait for the Sahib. The air up there was thick with yellow dust, stirred up by many feet. Coolies quarreled about the coming business. The echo of their words came down to the boats clustered below. Hawkers yelled their wares—hot tea and sweetmeats and betel nut to chew.

Again Hafiz had that nice feeling that something wonderful was going to happen. He did not remember the man who had been their tenant for six weeks last season. He had been too shy then to come out and look at him. Now he was excited to think that the man would soon be here. This time he would not be afraid to look.

Hafiz sat in the very tip of the bow and held a paddle. He could push with it and hold the boat steady. Or he could prevent another boat bumping into them. People were always crashing into each other. He felt very brave with his paddle while Abdullah was there, behind him on the middle seat.

Suddenly, over on the right, a louder noise

could be heard. All the boat folk looked in that direction. Two boats had crossed bows in the channel. One was a very fine *shikara* with fresh white curtains that had a red pattern. The other was a common one, with fish baskets. It smelled very bad. Under the curtains of the fine *shikara* sat Sayyad Khan, dressed in a beautiful cream wool embroidered coat. He was shouting at the fish man and shaking his coat out where a little water had splashed. The water at the Gate was very dirty and Sayyad Khan was plainly annoyed. He was telling off the generations of the fish man's family and the poor fellow looked terrified.

"The old fox!" exclaimed Abdullah softly, under cover of the noise. "I wonder what he is doing here. If he makes trouble for the father . . . !" Abdullah laid his paddle in the bottom of the boat. "Sit quietly, Small One, I will go up and tell the father."

Before Hafiz could say a word, Abdullah had leaped out of the boat, over his head. He stopped on the steps and said something to the policeman, who looked at Hafiz and nodded. Then Abdullah was up the steps and away. Hafiz felt his heart begin to pound double. Never before had they left him alone in the boat, not like this. He had to use both hands on his paddle now to keep the boat steady. And he knew he must stay in that place so they could load the Sahib's luggage easily.

Above in the road, the sound of motors and the smell of gasolene increased. The coolies set up a delighted shout which drowned out all other sounds. Hafiz looked up. He could just see, over the tops of the many heads along the railing, the shapeless bundles of luggage which he knew were on top of a motor bus.

While he was watching the road, a boat pulled up next Hafiz, almost pushing him out of his place, and there was Sayyad Khan, smiling smoothly at him. How had he been able to crowd in here when he had been so far out a little while ago? And his eyes were still angry even though he was smiling.

"Good morning, boy! Your father, where is he?"

Hafiz salaamed politely, but he didn't answer. Abdullah would have known what to say. But Abdullah was not there. He felt terribly alone. What if Sayyad Khan should push him out of his place?

But there was the policeman. He had seen. He motioned to the man paddling for Sayyad Khan. "Get out of here!" he ordered. "There is no more room. This boat came first. Go back to the middle of the stream!"

Someone was not afraid of the great Sayyad Khan! The law had spoken and the law had to be obeyed. The policeman looked at Hafiz and grinned. Hafiz salaamed, with one hand. He got back close to the steps again, and held the boat there carefully against the broken board.

Passengers from the motor bus began coming down the steps just then, and the boatmen all began crying their bargains.

"Sahib! Lady Sahib! Take my boat! Mine is very good boat! Don't look at his, take mine! See my boat, please. Just have one looking!" It was almost like a tune, a repeated chorus of joy in display, and at the same time an effort to beat the other fellow at renting.

A few of the new arrivals selected taxi-boats, and others chose to inspect houseboats. The crowd was gradually rowed away with much splashing. There was left standing on the last good step one lone Englishman. He was badly sunburned. He wore khaki-colored shorts and his shoes were dusty. He took off his sun helmet and wiped his face with a white handkerchief.

He paid no attention to anyone. The taxi boat-men gave up after a while.

Hafiz wondered where their Sahib was. He wished this one could be he. He liked this man's face. Maybe their tenant had not come, after all. Where were his father and Abdullah?

Up in the road the shouting was still going on. Coolies were fighting about luggage loads. The man on the steps moved over to the far side, opposite Hafiz, and took out a thick block of white paper from his pocket. Hafiz watched every move. He almost forgot to hold the boat steady. The man was drawing a picture!

The Englishman looked at all the boats. Hafiz realized again that theirs was a very plain one. What if their Sahib should decide to take Sayyad Khan's after he came? Could the father get another tenant now? How else would they pay the debt money? It was some comfort to the little boy to remember yesterday's work.

THE NEW TENANT ARRIVES

The *Blue Heron* was clean and ready.

Sayyad Khan stood up in his fine *shikara* and made a salaam to the man on the steps but the man did not look at him. He went on making his picture. Hafiz could see the pencil flying over the paper.

Then more people with their coolies came swarming down the steps and the shouting began all over again. The coolies had bedding rolls strapped on their backs, water jugs in their hands, and tin trunks or suitcases on their heads.

The lone man on the steps turned about and said something to the policeman who grinned and saluted smartly. Then he went back up to the road, pushing his way through the crowd coming down.

At the very last Abdullah came. "Did you see the Sahib?" he asked. "He is here. His suitcase was lost. We have it now."

Abdullah was carrying an enamel washbasin

that had a leather top and handle. Following him, a coolie had a tin trunk, a suitcase, golf clubs, a small leather case, and a bedding roll. The things were hung all over the man, so that Hafiz wondered how he could see where he was going.

Abdullah and the coolie put all the things in the boat. It took a little time because they argued about the best way to pile the stuff. Then the coolie would not take the money the Sahib had given for him. He said it was not enough. "I am a poor man, and the Sahib should give me more!"

"Another one!" Hafiz thought. "Everybody wants it! I want school fees. The father wants to pay his debt. The farmer wants it for some reason. And Sayyad Khan! Now why does he want it? He has a fine shop and wears nice clothes. Why should he want more?" The little boy sighed because he could not answer a question that no one has ever been able to explain.

The father came down the steps but the Sahib was still nowhere to be seen. The big man waved his hand to Hafiz. "Ah, Small One! Well done! Hold the boat a little longer!" He went back up the steps again.

How Hafiz did wish they would hurry up and finish! His arms had begun to ache. The water splashed in little waves against the steps as one boat after another drew away. There was plenty of room now. Sayyad Khan still had no customer.

Ah! There was the father, returning at last. He sat in the stern and picked up Abdullah's paddle. That helped. Hafiz could rest a little. As soon as Sayyad Khan saw the father, he had his boat brought nearer. The two men faced each other over the pile of luggage. Then Sayyad Khan waved one hand, and delicately rubbed thumb and forefinger together.

The father shook his head. "Not today!" he said shortly.

Sayyad Khan's eyes grew darker in the bright sunlight. All his yellow teeth showed. His smile was not nice.

"You promised, stupid!" His voice was growing loud. "Remember, you have mouths to feed!"

"And did you think the Sahib would pay me before he got out of his motor?"

Sayyad Khan threw out his hands. "But you do not need the Sahib's money! Pay me from that you have hidden away! Do you think I believed your story the other day? Bah!"

Hafiz' paddle moved and a great splash of water jumped into Sayyad Khan's *shikara*. The beautiful cream wool coat was quite wet. Sayyad Khan lost his temper completely. He shouted angrily, "Stupid boy! Attend to your boat!"

Some people up on the road heard. They stopped and looked down over the railing. Hafiz grasped the paddle tightly again. Would Abdullah never come? He stole a shy glance at Sayyad Khan. He was brushing away at his coat.

As Hafiz looked, the man's face changed and broke into smiles. He began an elaborate salaam. Then Hafiz saw Abdullah and the man who had made the picture coming down the steps. He must be their Sahib! The sketch block was put away, but Abdullah had the picture in his hand. Also he still carried the washbasin with the leather top. The handle went flat when the basin was set down. Hafiz hoped they would let him hold it.

The little boy stood up in his place and salaamed. The Sahib gravely returned his greeting. Abdullah helped hold the boat steady while he got in. Then Abdullah followed him and pushed the boat away from the steps.

The Sahib had not paid any attention to Sayyad Khan, except for a brief nod. When Hafiz looked for him, the *shikara* was slowly drifting away. Sayyad Khan had wasted his morning.

Abdullah sent their boat ahead with long easy strokes. Hafiz asked to see the picture. It was a funny one. All the boats at the Gate were in it, just as they had been that morning, and in the middle, looking fat and lazy under his canopy, was Sayyad Khan. The Sahib had seen him, after all!

The sun was high now. It was almost noon. Hafiz was hungry, and he wanted to go to sleep. He wished he had his basket of sweets. He sat down in the bottom of the boat between Abdullah's feet. He was not too sleepy to remember that if he stuck his own bare feet out from beneath his coat, the Sahib would see he was not wearing shoes.

When they were well out into the lake, away from the trees, there was no shade at all. The light on the water made his eyes blink so he shut them a couple of times to keep from squinting. He heard the new tenant ask:

"Was that rascal Sayyad Khan pestering you about money? Do you need money? I can give you rent today. Let him try any of his tricks this year!"

Hafiz did not hear his father's reply. He could feel a sigh coming, all the way up from his feet. Everything was going to be all right now. The father could pay something on the debt, and there might be some left for shoes. And it seemed the Sahib knew a lot about Sayyad Khan.

That nice feeling came again, before Hafiz went to sleep leaning against Abdullah's knee.

11

HAFIZ PLAYS BALL

ALTHOUGH HAFIZ WATCHED CAREFULLY ALL
that afternoon, he did not see the rent paid. No
one said anything about shoes, either. They
were all too busy to talk to him.

The little boats were waiting for him in the
pool by the willow root. He untied the *shikara*

and looked at his savings again. The three pieces were there safely, and quite dry. He thought about Sayyad Khan. The merchant had many boats. Why should he want to take their tenant away? The Sahib was here, however, and it was taking more of Abdullah's time to settle him in.

From the willow root it was easy to see much that was going on, but he went back to the *doonga* several times to get a drink. Rafia had more work today, too, because her mother was helping cook the Sahib's food.

Abdullah flew back and forth along the runway with covered dishes in his hands, giving the Sahib his lunch. The big brother looked very fine in his long white serving coat. It was new. The tailor had sewed it in the bazaar.

Hafiz tried to keep step with Abdullah but it was no use. The Sahib was hungry and he had to hurry.

The farmer and his coolie were working today in the corner of the field nearest the *doonga*. They did not call salaams, but they stopped several times to watch Abdullah.

The farmer's wife and another woman came in a boat. They pulled weeds all afternoon from the vegetable rows in the floating gardens. The ducks made a great fuss when the women came. They always did a lot of extra quacking if there were any unusual moving about, either on land or water.

After lunch was finished, Abdullah took off his long white coat and went away in the *shikara*. He was in a hurry and did not invite Hafiz to go along. The Sahib wanted the light-without-oil to be connected at once. Abdullah must go to the tax office for the paper.

When he came back, saying the paper would not be ready before a week, the Sahib said, "Nonsense!" He came down from the deck and went away with Abdullah. And they didn't ask Hafiz to go with them.

Hafiz suddenly felt very much alone and he did not like the feeling. His father was in the houseboat mending a hole in a windowscreen. The Sahib had said he did not like flies to come in. Hafiz was not permitted to go in there, either. Everything was very different already. He would have liked sitting on the steps that led to the roof. He wanted to look at the deep picture of the mountains and the clouds in the water. But the father said, "Nay! Nay!"

The little boy wandered back to the willow root. He stood and watched the two women in the garden opposite him. They were talking. Their tongues worked as fast as their hands. One of them had her baby with her. The little thing cried, so she scooped out a place for it in the soft earth, padded it with the weeds, and the baby went to sleep.

Hafiz wished he had a baby to play with. He would show Abdullah he could have fine times without him. When had the *shikara* gone away without Hafiz sitting in the middle, holding tight? Well, not many times, but sometimes, if it was very special business.

He started to jump from the willow root over to the place where the women were working. Maybe they would let him play with that baby. But the women yelled at him to go away, and the baby woke up and cried again.

The whole world was busy and nobody would talk. He wouldn't hurt their old baby. He went back to the *doonga*. Rafia gave him his basket of sweets and he sat out in the bow with it. From that good place he could watch for Abdullah to return.

Little bits of the leaves which formed the basket were chipping off. They were dry because he had kept it so long. The crumbled bits mixed with the sweets. The raisins and nut meats were all gone now, and the cocoanut squares, and the crisp crisscross rings. The large sticky ball with cheese inside was left. He had saved it for the last. He decided to eat it at once. There could not be a better time. He broke off some of the outside and ate it carefully. He got up and offered Rafia a piece but she shook her head. She was making supper bread. Her hands were in the dough. When he insisted, she opened her red mouth and he popped a bit inside. She laughed and Hafiz chuckled way down in his tummy.

He felt better after that, and even thought of saving a piece for Abdullah. But he changed his mind and after a while all of the big sticky sweet was gone. He poked around in the sugar crumbs and leaf bits at the bottom of the basket to see if he had missed anything. There was one small piece of nut meat and some cocoanut shreds. When he had eaten those, he threw the basket into the lake.

It floated away lightly on the water, until it was stopped, caught on a clump of marsh grass. Hafiz sighed. It had been the nicest present anyone had ever given him. He looked toward the bend. He did wish Abdullah would come back.

But the marsh hens were settling and a few bats had begun to fly before the *shikara* returned.

Hafiz was tired, so tired, from the long day. He did not say anything when the jingling sound of his mother's bracelets came out of the dark. She reached a hand down to him and he was glad to lean against her on the way in to supper.

Abdullah and his father talked late that night, but they said nothing about shoes. Hafiz would have heard, if they had. Abdullah said they had got the light permit after waiting a long time.

There were so many things to be done in the houseboat and *doonga* that a full week went by before new shoes could even be thought of. Hafiz had thought of them often. Every time he felt pebbles and twigs in the path he wished for shoes.

Each morning the Sahib had taken Abdullah and the *shikara* and they had gone off to the royal gardens to paint pictures. Hafiz was not invited to go, not once.

The little boats and the red ball helped. Rafia had found the forgotten ball and put it in the stores box. She offered it, instead of sweets, the next time Hafiz came wandering lonesomely into the cooking place.

He sat in the path and rolled the ball, cautiously. It went a little way and stopped. He was glad it did not roll in the water. He grew more used to the ways of rubber balls and began tossing it from the path to the *doonga*. When he grew tired of that, he looked about for a better place. Perhaps the roof of the houseboat? No, that was a little too high. The ball might stick in the railing. Or it might go on over into the water on the other side. He turned toward the land. The vegetable gardens where the women had worked the other day would be fine.

Hafiz stood by the willow root and tossed the ball above the little boats, into the green mass beyond. The ball bounced back. He tried again. It bounced back almost into his hand. What fun! He tossed it many times. Then, at last, he threw too hard. The ball did not bounce back. It lay hidden in the leaves.

What to do? He must get the ball. There was no one in sight. It was morning and everybody was busy. The houseboat was empty. The farmer and his coolie were not working in the field. He gathered up the hem of his long coat and sprang onto the willow root. It was an easy jump then to the floating garden. Could he find the ball?

When he stepped into the garden, it seemed a different place than it appeared, even from so short a distance away as the willow root. He could not remember the exact spot where the ball had fallen.

He parted the leaves and walked between plants, looking. At the far end of a row, when he had about given up finding his treasure, he saw it. But he also saw something else far more exciting. A baby! He was sure it was the one he had seen the day the Sahib came. It lay in a little scooped-out hollow among the plants. The ball was lying half hidden by the baby's shawl.

Hafiz had not seen the women come to the gardens to work that morning. But they must have been here, or the baby would not be lying there asleep. He leaned over and touched its cheek with one finger. The little thing opened its eyes and smiled at Hafiz. Then it yawned and he could see two small white teeth. This was a fine baby. How he did wish it was his little brother!

Someone should be here with the baby. If the women had asked him, he would have been glad to stay with it. Perhaps he ought to take it to the boat anyway. He sat there a long time before he could decide what to do.

If it were the farmer's baby . . . ! His eyes sparkled with a wonderful idea. He gathered the child up in his arms. To carry the ball, too, he tucked it down between himself and the baby. When he got to the edge of the garden he knew he could not jump back.

He laid the baby down where it could see him. He did not want it to cry. Then he tucked up his coat again and jumped across to the wil-

low root and then to the runway. There he tugged at the plank which led to the houseboat at the front door. He pulled it over to the willow root and slanted it down to the garden. It was just right. He ran down, picked up the baby and the ball again, and returned to the runway. The baby was enjoying all this activity. He gurgled and chuckled and spit all over Hafiz' coat. He fussed a little when Hafiz laid him down a second time. But it was only long enough to put the plank back in its place.

Then Hafiz had to decide where he would take the baby. The Sahib was not at home. His bed would be ready to sleep on, and soft.

Hafiz picked up the baby once more and hurried with him through the Sahib's front door and into the bedroom, beyond the dining room and the galley. The bed was ready, with the mosquito net rolled back neatly. Abdullah attended to that every morning. He laid the baby on the bed. The baby smiled and was ready to play. He lifted his fat little arms and Hafiz patted his hands together.

There were tiny bracelets almost sunk in the fat creases around the baby's wrists. His eyes were painted black with kohl to keep the flies away. He was clean and his shawl was fine. Somebody took care of this baby very well. That somebody would be hunting for it. Hafiz' eyes sparkled again. He wanted to play with the baby. But he wanted more to watch outside.

After a while the baby went to sleep again and Hafiz slipped away. He sat down in the bow of the *doonga*, very quietly. Rafia came out and asked if he felt all right. She said he looked as if he had been out in the sun too long.

"Where is the red ball?" she asked.

Hafiz had forgotten the ball. He remembered bringing it with him from the garden.

"I left it over there." He waved vaguely in the general direction of the runway and the houseboat. He could hear Rafia telling her mother that she thought Hafiz was sick. The mother came to him and felt his head. She, too, asked if he felt all right. Of course he did! She went jingling back to the cooking place and Hafiz sat on, wondering what would happen first.

12

AN UNFINISHED ARGUMENT

THE SUN WAS ALMOST OVERHEAD BEFORE there was any movement in the quiet waters of the channel. Hafiz had wished for the tenth time that he had brought the red ball with him, when he saw Sayyad Khan's boat at the bend. It came closer before he noticed his father sitting on the floor with Sayyad Khan. It was not the freshly curtained *shikara* but the shop boat again.

Hafiz salaamed politely when the boat stopped. The father stepped aboard the *doonga*. Sayyad Khan was all smiles this morning, and the ugly glitter in his eyes was gone. Hafiz looked at his father. The big man seemed very still inside.

Sayyad Khan sat on in his boat, making no move to go. He looked very handsome this morning and knew it. His turban was perfectly wound. His beard had been carefully brushed and trimmed. His coat showed no signs of the splashing it had received a week ago.

"Shall I leave the rug?" he asked finally, when all the usual words had been said.

"Nay!" said the father. "The Sahib is not here. He has gone to the far marshes to paint. I will not be responsible for anything left in his houseboat."

"You call it his boat!" exclaimed Sayyad Khan. "Have you sold it to him?"

"It is his while he rents it," the father answered shortly.

"I see," said the merchant. "And do you not see that I trust all in this boat?" he insisted. "I know the rug will be safe." His voice was smooth.

"Yes, the rug would be safe but we would not." The father's voice was not smooth. It sounded like a boat grinding on a pebbly beach.

There was nothing to be gained by arguing when the father said "Nay!" Hafiz knew that and Sayyad Khan must learn it. So the fine merchant had to tell his boatman to push off. They swung slowly around, into the channel again. The shop boat itself seemed unwilling to leave.

When the visitor was out of sight, Rafia came out with the pipe. The big man thanked her and sat down in the bow by Hafiz. He sighed, a deep one, and tucked the little boy against him in the crook of his right arm. It had been a long time since they had sat alone like this.

The water in the pipe gurgled pleasantly. The sun felt warm and Hafiz took off his cap and rubbed his head. The noon gun boomed from the Fort. Hafiz could see the white puffs of smoke against the blue sky. It was very still and peaceful.

After a while the pipe stem was swung away, and Hafiz' father talked. "So, my Small One! Now that that poor man, Sayyad Khan, has had something on account, we shall go to the shops, you and I. Perhaps tomorrow we shall go, if the Sahib does not need the boat."

Hafiz could feel his heart beating strongly. Shoes at last? He had waited long and long.

His father spoke again. "Somehow I think the Sahib will not need the boat tomorrow. I will tell him a thing, and he will paint from the top of the houseboat. Why go to the marshes or the royal gardens? There is much to be seen by staying at home." He chuckled, and Hafiz did, too.

"What shops?" asked Hafiz. He wanted to hear the words.

"Going to the sho-ops
Buying shoes for Hafiz."

Those were the words his heart said, and they made a little tune.

The father was smoking again, long puffs. He squinted against the sunlight on the water. Another boat was coming down the channel and it was sending little waves dancing toward the *doonga*. The noon sunlight gave them bright tips.

Hafiz looked up at his father. The same brightness was in his eyes. They twinkled as he answered.

"Well, first there is an errand at the wood-carver's shop, to take a gift for that baby having your name. We had no money to buy one on his name day."

Hafiz' heart beat a little faster, but he sat quietly.

"Then I must have a word with the carpenter, two streets in from Third Bridge. The Sahib wants a shelf built above his bed for the clock."

Clocks, what did they matter, Hafiz thought. People went to bed for sleeping, and there was the gun at the Fort for time. What about shoes?

"What else?" Hafiz asked, aloud. He would not give up hope yet.

"For the rest, in the street of the leather workers we shall see what we can find for two little Kashmiri feet that are now quite bare!"

The father reached down and pulled one of Hafiz' feet up. He held it in his hand. "This nail is torn. This toe is scratched. This one has a sliver. And all are muddy!"

Hafiz laughed. He wiggled his toes in his father's hand. "Those are my feet that are bare. It is my feet that will have new shoes!" He shouted it.

"Truly said!" the father remarked. He smoked again. The pipe bubbled and the coals glowed. The sweet odor of the smoke dulled the smell of water and leaves, of fish and ducks and cooking food.

"My father, there is a thing to be said!" Hafiz spoke after a little silence. He felt very bold, mentioning that thing, but his heart beat heavily. It almost hurt. The pipe was still, while the father waited.

"When you were a little boy, did you go to school?"

The pipe was set completely away. The smoking was over for now. "Nay, it was not the fashion when I was a little boy. It is not very much the fashion still."

"Abdullah went to school."

"Yes, Abdullah went to school. We needed a little learning in the family. He is the first son!"

"Why may I not go to school?" Hafiz wanted to hear those words, too. They were even more important than hearing the promise of the precious shoes.

If the father was surprised, it did not sound in his voice. The little boy's heart was more quiet.

"The mother would never hear of it. She and Rafia need you at home. I need you."

"It is for women to stay at home," Hafiz objected. "I am a man now. You said it when I helped carry books. I want to go to school."

There, it was out, said in real words.

The father slowly rubbed both the rough, bare little feet while he talked, grown-up fashion, man to man.

"It costs money for school fees. We never know where we will tie up in the season. We might be far away. There are many reasons."

Hafiz did not say anything but he wiggled his feet again. Those were not good reasons, except the money.

"Why not be a strong boatman?" his father argued. "You do not need to go to school for that. Men who have learned, sit at counters and write things in big books. They work in the post office. They work at the bank. You wouldn't like to stay indoors all the time?"

Hafiz nodded yes, vigorously. It sounded wonderful. But not every school man did those things. Abdullah did not.

"But Abdullah stays with us!" he said, aloud.

"Ah, yes!" said the father, smiling behind his beard. "That is different. Abdullah wanted to go in the Army. But he must read the English letters for me. He must go with the tenants to the shops and the gardens. He must do the accounts, so that we will not be cheated for the rice. All those things."

"But I want to go to school, too. At school there will be other little boys," Hafiz insisted. "But not with my name!" he added.

"Yes, other little boys would be there!" the father agreed thoughtfully. "I am sorry you have had to play alone so much since the Sahib came. But Abdullah has a fine surprise for you. That will help a little. You will see!"

Hafiz knew it would do little good to ask for Abdullah's secret, so he waited for what else his father might say.

"You heard me tell Sayyad Khan the boat is the Sahib's for now. That is why you could not come in with me when I mended the screen. And you cannot go in the *shikara* with Abdullah and the Sahib unless you are invited. That is why you have had to play alone. It is very hard to understand some of these things."

"I could learn understanding in the school," Hafiz argued.

His father laughed at that, but Hafiz thought guiltily about the baby. He had almost forgot about it while they had been talking. But taking the baby in there was not really playing in the houseboat. He had gone in only to put the little baby in a safe place. Then he thought of the farmer and wanted to laugh. That would be a surprise for everybody, if the baby were his.

They heard voices in the houseboat, forward. Abdullah and the Sahib had returned, from the other direction. Abdullah appeared, presently, in the *shikara*. He threw the painter over the hook and leaped carelessly aboard the *doonga*. Hafiz watched as he never tired doing. He wondered if they taught boys to leap on boats, at school.

Almost immediately there were shouts from the Sahib. "Ai hai!" Abdullah said, and hurried into his white coat before running along the path.

When he came back to them, still running, he had a queer look on his face. "The Sahib says," he reported, panting, "that there is a baby on his bed. Somebody must come and get it at once!"

The father stood up so suddenly that Hafiz was spilled, kerflump, on the deck. "Ai hai!" was his comment. "A baby! Whose baby? How could it get on the Sahib's bed? Is it all right?"

"I did not see the baby, my father, but the Sahib says it is sleeping and he is afraid it will wake up and cry."

167

Rafia and her mother, feeling the excitement, had come out. The mother said, "I will see!" and followed Abdullah, to fetch the unwanted visitor.

Hafiz sat very still. He scarcely dared breathe. His idea did not seem quite so wonderful now. What would his father say?

He had no time to think farther. Just then a boat came sliding in between the runway and the lake bank. In it were the farmer and the two women who had worked in the floating gardens several days before. The farmer was talking angrily and paid no attention to Hafiz and his father. One of the women was crying.

Hafiz stood up to watch where they were going. The farmer sculled the boat close up to the garden and the crying woman got out. She went straight to the place where he had found the baby. Of course it was not there. She screamed and beat her head with her hands.

The farmer shouted at her. Hafiz did not understand what he said. In no time at all the ducks were adding their excited quacking to the confusion.

The other woman in the boat suddenly stood up and pointed to the runway. Hafiz looked, too. There was his mother with the baby in her arms. The woman in the garden stopped crying. She began to run between the rows of vegetables. A bean vine tripped her and she fell down. The farmer picked up his other paddle and gave it to the woman in the boat with him. She sat down and he pushed the boat away from the bank.

Hafiz would have liked to go to bed now. How had Rafia known that he was sick? He felt cold and then hot, and his heart beat so fast he could not breathe.

The woman in the garden picked herself up and ran again. When she reached the place where Hafiz had jumped to the willow root, she jumped, too. She ran along the path behind Hafiz's mother, calling to her to give up the baby. That woke the baby and he howled.

The farmer's boat appeared round the end of the *doonga*. He stopped in the very place where he himself had once tumbled in the water. He began talking but his words ran into each other and they could not understand him.

Then things began to happen almost too fast to see all at one time. Hafiz' father walked over to the farmer to hear better. The woman followed his mother onto the *doonga* and snatched the crying baby out of her arms. She talked fast, too. People were all talking at once. The farmer yelled loudest. It sounded like the bazaar. Hafiz crept over and seized tight hold of a handful of his mother's coat.

It did not help any that Abdullah came just then from the houseboat. He had the red ball

in his hand. He walked straight to Hafiz, hiding behind his mother. The noise was so loud no one else heard what he said. Hafiz was glad for that.

"The Sahib found this in his bedroom. It was on the bed with the baby. There was mud on his rug." Abdullah looked down at the dried mud on Hafiz' feet. He did not smile.

Hafiz held out his hand for the ball, but Abdullah would not give it to him. "Nay!" said he. "Not until we hear the story. Perhaps it is a mistake to leave you at home!" He walked away. He wouldn't even stand there.

The father turned away from the farmer. He clapped his hands together and shouted, too. "Silence! Let peace be in my house!"

All the talking and crying and shouting stopped. Only the ducks still quacked and swam about in little darts and jerks.

"Now then," said the father. "What is this

disturbance about? Can you not live quietly with your neighbors? We have done nothing."

"You have done nothing? You think it is nothing to hide my baby?" The farmer nearly fell into the water again.

"We hide a baby? I never saw that baby before. It is a nice baby, and if it is yours you should see that the women take better care of it." Hafiz felt better and wanted to laugh. He hid his chuckle in his mother's skirt. His father was so quiet and the farmer had thoroughly lost his temper.

"I did take care of him," screamed the woman holding the baby. "I left him to make the food. He was all right. He was asleep. When I came back he was gone." She hugged the baby to her so tightly that it frightened him and he yelled again. How that baby could yell when he tried!

Hafiz felt his mother's hand on his head. He

174

came out from behind her skirt. Abdullah was watching him. Was this the right time to tell, and claim his reward? But no, his father was speaking again.

"I should report this to the police. The Kuptan Sahib should know about it. I have a guest. He finds a baby in a place you have no right to enter. He is disturbed. There is the law!"

"Law!" screamed the farmer. "Police! I should report you for stealing a baby!"

Hafiz looked at Abdullah, who nodded. He crossed the deck and stood near his father but not at his side. He felt alone. This thing he had done was . . . He said, "My father did not steal your baby. My mother did not steal your baby. I did not steal your baby. It was left on the ground. I found it. There was no one to take care of it. All were gone." Hafiz made a sweeping gesture with his hands that seemed to say he and the baby had been alone in a whole universe.

"I put that nice baby in a safe place," he went on. Then he folded his arms across his body the way he had seen the policeman do at Dal Gate. "You should give me a rupee!"

The farmer stared at him. It was very quiet. Abdullah grinned. Hafiz went to him and claimed the red ball from his hand. Still the farmer was silent. His jaws worked but no sound came. Hafiz bounced the ball once.

"For finding the baby, one rupee!" he said again. "I need the money!"

Then the farmer found his voice. "You . . . need money!" he gasped. "Give you a rupee? Beggar! A rupee, that is owed to me!" He would have struck Hafiz with his paddle, if Abdullah had not stepped forward quickly.

"Everything is even, don't you think?" he asked. "You saved him, and he has kept your baby safely. Take your family and go!"

The farmer's wife hurried across the *doonga* and stepped down into the boat. Abdullah helped her. Hafiz did not want them to go. Why was the farmer so angry? He was always angry nowadays. It was a nice baby. He would have liked playing with it.

As he paddled away, the farmer had the last word. "You have money to buy foreign toys and cannot give me a token for kindness, or pay lawful debts," he taunted.

A foreign toy! Hafiz bounced the ball again. The farmer saw. He went away shouting threats of what he would do. Finally Hafiz' mother brought a tall vegetable basket and set it bottom side up in the bow. That meant the argument would be finished another day. When the farmer saw the basket he stopped yelling.

"Ah, woman, that one will never be satisfied until he gets his token," the father remarked. "What a sorry thing!"

Hafiz had not looked at his father yet. Now he felt the big man's hand on his chin, lifting it up, and up, until their eyes met.

"But this child . . ." the father went on as if he were still talking to the mother . . . "this child is right. He needs understanding." Only Hafiz and his father knew what that meant.

In the late afternoon Abdullah went to the post office for the Sahib's letters and newspaper. He took Hafiz with him, sitting in the middle seat of the *shikara*, very quietly.

"Why did you do it, Small One? Can't you keep out of trouble?"

"For the fees," Hafiz answered soberly. "School fees. I want to go to the River School."

Abdullah stopped paddling and looked at him thoughtfully. Then he smiled. "Is that why you have not spent your coppers and the silver you found?"

Hafiz nodded. Abdullah started paddling again. "It is good to save," he said slowly; "they teach you that," he added. "But you will need much more. It takes many rupees to pay the fees at my school."

"But you went, Abdullah!"

"Yes . . . I went. But you do not know how I went. I think you should know now. The father . . . borrowed the fees from Sayyad Khan."

There was a little silence. Hafiz waited.

"That is why I could not go in the Army. I must help the father pay it back. Now you know."

The boat pushed on through the smooth water. The paddle made little swishing sounds. Nothing more was said. Hafiz sighed. So many things to be paid for! Everybody wanted pay for something, and somebody was always paying!

13

THE PROMISE IS KEPT

IF EVER A MORNING WERE MADE TO GO SHOP-
ping in, that one was. Hafiz was up long before
the others. He went out and sat in the bow,
waiting. The rest of the family were taking
their time about starting this important day,
he thought. Of a truth, the father had said they
would go to the shops, if the Sahib did not need

the boat. But surely he would not! Oh, surely!

It was chilly in the early morning. The deck boards were still damp from the dew. Hafiz tucked the hem of his coat in round his feet, and stopped shivering.

Solomon's Mountain made a long blue shadow on the water, a shadow that reached almost to the edge of the marsh. The king-fishers dived and splashed, hunting fish. From somewhere far away, but clearly, came the well-song. Hafiz liked that sound. Someone else was up early this morning, and at work.

Several boats went by in the channel. They were loaded down with water plants for cattle food. A small boy, no older than Hafiz himself, sat in the very tip of one of them. A girl not as tall as Rafia was standing up to pole the boat. The children stared at each other as long as it was in sight. Hafiz wished he could play with that boy. He wondered if he went to school.

After a long time, Abdullah came out with the Sahib's early tea tray. Hafiz followed him along the runway. He stopped to look at the little boats. The walnut shell one was full of water. The pineneedle sailor was quite wet. The *Silver Moon* looked tidy and trim. But he checked the floor beneath a floor and found the cargo still there.

Abdullah came back just as the last loop was tied. He was grinning. "Ho, little brother! Come with me! Here is news! The Sahib does not need the boat today. And he has sent you a pocketpiece!"

Hafiz jumped up and ran ahead of Abdullah to the *doonga*. Now they really could go to the bazaar! If the Sahib had needed the boat today . . . It was too awful to think about.

As they reached the cooking place, Rafia took the last round of bread out of the ashes.

"Breakfast, Rafia!" Hafiz shouted. "We are

going to the bazaar and I've got a pocketpiece. The Sahib sent it to me! What is a pocketpiece, Abdullah? Where is it? Let me see it!"

The little boy was almost too excited to eat his bread. He would not sit down with the others. He danced around Abdullah while the big boy pretended to search all through his clothes for the gift. He looked sad when he opened his hands to show there had been nothing in his pockets.

Rafia spoiled Abdullah's fun. "Is this it, Abdullah? Here is a two-anna bit on the tray."

Hafiz swooped down on her as she knelt on the floor in front of the tea tray. There lay a small piece of silver, only a little larger than a big drop of dew. Everybody laughed. It was affectionate laughter, but Hafiz put his hands behind his back and refused to touch it. If they laughed it must be a joke.

Abdullah picked up the little coin. "Nay,

Small One, it is all right. This is the pocket-piece. One does not see these much nowadays. It is to be carried about with you for good luck. Are you not having good luck already? To be going to the shops with the father?"

Hafiz held out his hand. Then he drew it back. "I have no pocket," he said solemnly.

Abdullah said to Rafia, "A man should have pockets," as if it were her fault that there were no pockets in Hafiz' coat.

Rafia tossed her long braids back over her shoulder. "A pocket you shall have, Little Brother, before this day is done."

Hafiz wondered how that could be managed. It would be very nice to carry the lucky piece with him to the shops. Not to spend, oh, no! Just to hold.

Rafia opened the stores box. That marvelous hideaway held many things. She searched in its farthest corner. Out came a piece of black thread. She felt along the edge of her dress collar and took out a needle. Hafiz watched her thread the needle. What was she going to do?

"Come, Hafiz, I am ready. This will be as good as a pocket until we can make a better one. Stand still!"

She lifted the edge of Hafiz' wide, loose sleeve. She broke a thread between the outside and the lining, making a little opening. She held up the coin.

"See! I shall sew it securely in the seam. You can feel it there all day. Some other time I can make a real pocket. But today you may carry the lucky piece wherever you go."

Hafiz stood quietly while the sewing went on. Rafia stitched all around the edge of the little coin, so it could not slip out. She closed the break in the seam again. It was safe. There was a little lump in the seam, but no one would know what made it.

Each of the family in turn was invited to feel that little lump in Hafiz' sleeve. It was a wonderful pocket.

Rafia and her mother were quite contented to stand together in the bow of the *doonga* to watch Hafiz and his father start away to Third Bridge. The women were used to staying at home.

Hafiz sat in his place on the middle seat and looked about him. Abdullah had come along to take a paddle. When they reached the shops, he would have business for the Sahib. The purchase of the shoes and the other errands would be left to his father and Hafiz, alone.

They slipped gently along through the quiet water. They did not meet many boats. It was too early, in this part of the lake. But there were many birds about. Butcher birds were nesting and now and then a gay orange male flew down, searching for worms and insects in the reeds.

Hafiz liked the paradise flycatcher best. He always hoped to see a white one. There were plenty of copper-colored young males to be seen, but when an old white one flew down the marsh, even a little boy could feel it was different and lovely. The two long tail feathers floated in long scallops like a streamer of cloud.

The way to the river took them past a huge *chenar* tree by an old barn. The tree was a favorite nesting place for the flycatchers. This morning Hafiz was disappointed. Although he looked back as long as the tree was in sight, the birds did not appear.

It was the beginning of summer. All the leaves had come out on the trees. Honeysuckle was in bloom, trailing its fragrant stems in the lake. Usually Hafiz begged to go slowly in this part of the trip. Today he thought it was taking twice as long to go. Abdullah knew a short

cut, however, which they followed after passing the flycatcher tree, and it was not long before they reached steps, where the boat was
tied.

At the top they came into a road leading to
Third Bridge. The floor of the bridge was made
of narrow boards fitted together. There were
long planks down the middle for motor cars.
Down here in the city many people were stirring. There was a constant stream of them,
crossing the bridge in both directions. A coolie
woman had a bundle of firewood on her head.
A washerman led a donkey carrying two huge
bundles of laundry. They stuck out on either
side and people had to get out of the way. The
bridge shook when they walked on it.

Hafiz held his father's hand tightly. He did
not like the shaking feeling. Abdullah had gone
ahead, and they could not see him now because
of the crowd. He would meet them at the boat

when all the morning's business was finished.

The wood-carver's shop faced the river. The work stopped there when Hafiz and his father climbed to the loft. The men smiled at Hafiz. Here he was not shy. These men were all his friends. The wood-carver sat down with the father to have a friendly smoke. He asked if Hafiz wanted to see the new baby. Hafiz decided he did not. He still could not quite forgive it for having his name. He did not understand why his father and the wood-carver smiled when he refused.

In the chips and shavings of wood on the floor he found a small block which was shaped a little like a boat. If two corners were rounded, it would look even more like one. He showed it to the man nearest him.

"See this?" All the workmen looked. "It is almost like a boat!"

The man picked up a tool. "Do you want another boat? I will cut it for you."

Hafiz nodded and handed over the little block. Two curled shavings came away, following the curve of the sharp knife. The piece of wood looked more like a boat. Again the sharp tool flashed. It bit a wide piece out of the inside of the block. Hafiz saw every move of the workman's long, slender hands. A shaving here, a little chip there, made the likeness more true every minute. Then there was a little smoothing with an agate tip and Hafiz found in his hand a tiny *shikara* with seats carved out. He salaamed deeply, and all his white teeth flashed in his smile.

He ran to his father, to show the boat. He salaamed the wood-carver for it. The wood-carver nodded at the workman, who was watching. The others laughed, and then they all picked up their tools again and began chipping away at their craft. One man was making a tray. Another was carving the lid of a box with the lovely iris pattern of Kashmir. There were no marks on the wood, and Hafiz had never understood how they made the flowers, though he had watched often.

"The flowers are in his heart," the wood-carver said once when Hafiz asked.

He was quite willing to go when the time came. His father stood up and drew from his sleeve a small parcel. That was the gift for the baby. Hafiz had forgot for the moment why they had come. The wood-carver salaamed, giving thanks for the present and in farewell.

Out in the street, the father took long steps. They had stayed too long at the wood-carver's and must hurry now. Hafiz carried the boat in one hand and held onto his father's coat with the other.

When they had walked a short way, Hafiz heard a loud sound. It was like the humming of bees, many bees. The noise became louder. It was somewhere above them. No one else in the street was paying any attention. He looked up.

Through the open windows of a room on the upper floor of a shop building, Hafiz could see many boys, sitting in rows. They were reading from books, aloud and at the top of their voices. The sound went high and died down, as they reached the end of a line. Then it rose again, like music.

"What is that, my father? What are those boys doing?"

The father laughed. "That is a school. How would you like to go there?"

Hafiz shook his head. He stumbled in the street because he was looking back at the boys.

"That is where I ought to send you. Those boys are learning the Koran, as all good Moslems should. They read all day long. They learn to say it without the book."

"I should not like it," said Hafiz, flatly. "They play ball at Abdullah's school. That is where I want to go."

"So!" said his father. "Well . . . one thing at a time. Today it is shoes."

Truly, today's chief business for Hafiz was shoes. He looked at the men walking in the street. Nearly all had shoes, great, stiff, heavy ones, or thin slippers without backs that flapped when they walked. He did not want his shoes to make that kind of noise. But he would not mind if they squeaked. If they did, folk would know he had new ones.

The carpenter's shop, two streets in from the river, was shut. No one could tell them when he would return. Hafiz was glad. Now, now they could go to the street of the leather workers.

They could smell that street before they came to it. It was a strong odor. Some shops used leather that had not been well tanned. But, oh, the beautiful shoes! Hafiz could not look hard enough. All the shops had open fronts and in every one there were rows and rows and shelves and shelves of shoes. The shelves reached to the top of each shop.

There were big shoes and little shoes. Some were small enough for a very little child. The big ones looked large enough for a giant, maybe. There were plain ones and embroidered ones, and some had gold patterns stamped on their toes. There were green ones and red ones. There were plain leather-colored ones. Hafiz was speechless.

They walked along the street until they came to the special shop the father was looking for. He knew the owner. The man sat in the middle of the shop on the floor and let his helper hand down the shoes. He wore spectacles half-way down his nose. He looked at Hafiz over the

top of them and waved his hand.

"Come in, come in," he invited. "You bring me good luck. You are my first customer to-day."

Hafiz knew what that meant. They would get a good price.

There were two short steps leading up to the shop. Hafiz climbed them, never taking his eyes off the rows of shoes. But when he was inside, he could not say what he wanted. He truly did not know.

The shopkeeper motioned to his helper to bring shoes. Hafiz sat down and stuck his feet out, straight in front of him on the floor. The helper handed down a pile of red shoes. They were something like his old ones with pointed tips. A pair was chosen to try on. Hafiz put his feet in them. They were too big. But against the shiny bright red leather he had seen his muddy feet. He tried to scrape off the mud with the hem of his coat. He felt better then, even though the helper said there were no red ones his size.

Next a pile of plain leather ones was set on the floor by Hafiz. They were stitched with white thread and had no long curling tips. Hafiz did not like them. He did not want to try them on. The shopkeeper looked at the father, who shook his head. So the helper took those away.

High up on the next shelf were three pairs of small green shoes, set apart by themselves. They were handed down. The shopkeeper looked at Hafiz' foot. He measured, so, with his hand. He selected a shoe, bent the stiff sole, and rubbed the leather until it was softer. He put it on Hafiz' foot. Hafiz stood up. The shoe stayed on. It was not tight. It did not fall off. It was just right.

The toes of this pair were stitched in gold

thread. They had curling, pointed tips. One extra thickness of leather made small heels. They were beautiful shoes.

The shopkeeper rubbed the other shoe until it, too, was soft. Hafiz put it on. He slid his feet back and forth on the worn floor matting. These were the right shoes. He looked up at his father and smiled.

The father spoke aloud for the first time. "So, you think these are the right ones? Green shoes, with tips?"

Hafiz nodded. He could not talk. He felt too happy.

The shopkeeper and the father began to bargain about the price. They did not hurry. They were both enjoying it. Hafiz sat down to wait, and the helper asked if he wanted to wear the shoes. Hafiz shook his head.

So the helper brought a piece of old newspaper and wrapped the shoes. Each shoe was wrapped, then they were laid together, one on top of the other, toe fitted into heel, and a flat package was made.

The discussion of the price ended. Both men seemed satisfied. Hafiz heard the jingle of money. He could not see how much it was, but he knew now that the shoes were really his. He stood up and salaamed, his father first, then the shopkeeper. The helper salaamed, too. Everybody was happy.

In the street Hafiz clutched his parcel tightly. It took both hands. His father carried the little boat for him. He also held one of the wide sleeves of Hafiz' coat, so they could not be separated in the crowded street. Hafiz thought of the pocketpiece. Had it brought him the beautiful green shoes? No, they were meant for him anyway, they fitted his feet so perfectly. They had been waiting on their shelf all this time.

Abdullah was already at the boat. He saw the parcel at once and suggested that Hafiz lay it in the bottom of the boat. But the little boy refused.

"I can sit one time without holding on," he said firmly. "When we reach the *doonga,* then I shall show you a thing. But for now the parcel should stay with me."

"I saw Sayyad Khan," Abdullah told them, after they had begun the return journey.

"And what had he to say?" asked the father.

"He wants the red ball. He says it belongs to his child."

"But how could that be?"

"He thinks it was rolled in a rug he brought for the Sahib to see last summer."

It was well Hafiz had the new shoes to make that moment easier. Give up the beautiful red ball!

"That red ball is mine. We found it!" Hafiz

objected. His voice trembled.

"How does Sayyad Khan know we have it?"

The father's hand was comforting on Hafiz' shoulder.

"Oh, the farmer, my father! Who else could know? He probably owes Sayyad Khan money, too, and Sayyad Khan is having a good time with all of us." Abdullah's voice was hard. "I wish I had never gone to school!" he added.

"Peace, boy! Don't say that! Your fees have been a wise spending. You will see!" the father urged. "We will finish the paying one day! Let us have one more good season!"

The big man patted Hafiz again, sitting there so straight, holding his precious parcel.

"Meantime the child's toy is another thing. I will ask the Sahib. He will say truly what we should do. I do not think Hafiz will be made to give it up."

"I splashed Sayyad Khan's coat," said Hafiz

abruptly. He had not thought of it again, until now.

"That is only a small part of it, my son. Sayyad Khan is greedy. He also loves power. That is a very bad thing in his hands, but it can also be a very good thing."

The father sighed somewhere far behind his beard, and nothing more was said. They were almost home.

14

HAFIZ GOES TO A BOAT RACE

HAFIZ TRIPPED ON HIS COAT, HE WAS IN SUCH
haste to climb aboard the *doonga*. He fell on
the deck. The parcel was still in his hand when
he got up, but his coat was ripped. The hem
hung in a long loop.

He was a sorry sight for Rafia when she appeared in the door. But she laughed, and he decided it was funny, too. The tears that had been so close because of the news about the ball, changed to eager words.

"See my shoes, Rafia! There were many, but one pair was for me! And I've got a boat, a new one!" His eyes shone.

"Why did you not wear the shoes, coming home?" Rafia demanded. She took the little boy's hand so he would not trip again, and led him in to the cooking place. Abdullah and the father were close behind them. The mother was stirring something at the low stove.

Hafiz looked down at his feet. "My feet were muddy!" he explained.

"So!" said Rafia. "For new shoes you must make clean the feet, is that it?" Hafiz nodded, grinning.

"But first, before that, and before you fall

down again, off comes this torn coat," she ordered.

The little coat was pulled up over his head. Getting it off was a slow process because he would not put the package down. After one arm was out, he transferred the shoes to the other hand. When he emerged from beneath the coat, he sat down and began unwrapping the shoes.

Rafia seemed more interested in the coat. She spread it out on the floor and pushed the torn edges together. She shook her head over the problem. But when Hafiz brought the shoes out of the last paper, she was ready to exclaim and admire the purchase with the others. The shoes were passed round, from hand to hand, Hafiz never taking his eyes from his precious property.

"Now you will have shoes to wear when you go to the races tomorrow," Rafia remarked, in a little silence.

"Ah, ah, Rafia!" began Abdullah, but his warning was too late. Hafiz had heard. He flung himself on Abdullah, who nearly lost his balance.

"Races, Abdullah? At Gagribal? The River School races? Can I go?" He faced his father. "Is that the surprise? Oh! Oh!"

"It is, if the Sahib does not want the boat." Abdullah made the half-promise, but Hafiz was already planning.

He picked up the shoes and put one on each hand. Then he did a little dance, round and round, clapping the shoes together to keep time.

> "Going to the races,
> Wearing new green sho-oes,"

he sang, to a tune of his own.

The mother interrupted. She reached out

and grasped his arm and the dancing came to an abrupt end. "How can you go to the races without a coat?"

Hafiz stared at the torn coat spread out on the floor. "But I have others," he objected. "Though there are no pockets for my pocket-piece. Let me go without a coat! It is warm now!" he urged.

His mother would not hear of it. "It might not be warm tomorrow!"

Rafia had the stores box open and was rummaging through its tumbled collection. She held up one of the coats he had worn the day he fell in the lake. It was clean, but, as Hafiz said, it had no pocket.

"Make me a pocket, Rafia?" he asked and gave her his most beguiling smile. "You said you would," he reminded her.

"But not all in one day, and I did not say 'tomorrow.'" Rafia was doubtful until she saw

her mother's consenting nod.

Abdullah got up from the floor. It was time to serve the Sahib's lunch. As he slowly fastened the wide belt of his white table coat, he gazed dreamily at Hafiz who still wore the new shoes on his hands. "When I come back, we will clean those feet," he announced solemnly.

"Nay," said Hafiz. "Not just my feet, Abdullah. I want all of me clean. I will have a clean coat, with a pocket in it. I want a clean shirt, too, and fresh pajamas to go with my clean feet. All of me should be clean." He set the shoes on the floor. He put his hand on his head and swept it down his body, leaning over to touch his feet. "All of me," he repeated.

Abdullah put his hand over his mouth to hide the sudden grin.

"We've got a little Lord Sahib in the cook-boat," he remarked to his mother. She frowned severely to hide her own amusement and motioned him out with his tray.

"There are too many people in here," she continued, when he had gone. "Out, all of you!"

Rafia had been busy at the fireplace and now she had the water in her father's pipe steaming nicely. Hafiz followed him out to the deck while the mother and Rafia held their domestic conference. Boxes were opened, their lids were banged shut again, and there was much laughter. It sounded as if Hafiz might have the clean shirt and perhaps the new pocket, too.

At two o'clock next day the *shikara* was headed toward the upper lake. Hafiz sat on the middle seat. His feet were stuck straight out in front of him, so that the beautiful new shoes could be the better seen. One hand was pushed down deep into the pocket which Rafia had sewed. It was wonderful to have a real pocket that he could put his hand in. He liked the feel of the place where Rafia had fastened the lucky piece in the pocket seam.

With his other hand, Hafiz occasionally reached up to feel his head. He wore a small turban! He could not believe it yet, so he had to touch it to make it real. He was a little dizzy with his fortune. To begin with, one did not get shoes often. Some boys had never worn shoes, Abdullah said. The pocket and the turban were curry on his rice.

This morning Rafia had called him in after breakfast. She held a piece of white cloth in her hand. Abdullah was there, too, and before Hafiz had known what was happening, they had wound the cloth round his head, the way Abdullah and his father wore theirs. Afterward, Abdullah had held him out over the boat edge so he could see himself in the clear water.

His head felt hot and for a moment he wished for the loose comfort of his old cap. But he wouldn't have taken the turban off for anything.

The family had stood on the deck and watched Hafiz and Abdullah get in the boat. Hafiz gave them a deep salaam, both palms together above his heart. As they passed the houseboat, Hafiz saw the Sahib on the roof. He was making a big picture. He came to the railing. Abdullah raised his hand and said, "S'laam, Sah'b!", very crisp and businesslike, and after a moment Hafiz had shyly done the same. This was a very good Sahib indeed, Hafiz thought. For two days he had not needed the boat.

There was much noise and color at Gagribal. On regatta day it looked very different from the usual quiet little basin at the corner of the upper lake. It was a perfect spot for boat races.

From the treetops at either side of the narrow entrance to the basin, a rope was stretched. This was the starting point and the finish line.

Along the rope were many flags, the Kashmir State, Union Jack, and various school house pennants. They blew back and forth gaily. They were a double row, with their bright colors reflected in the water. Hafiz had never seen so much massed all in one place and he could not decide which he wanted to look at more, the flags or the crowd.

Abdullah saw a good place, among friends, near the starting line. There was still room for one more boat, so he drew in and pushed the stern hard into the lake bank. Then he sat on the middle seat with Hafiz.

There were many boats moored in rows along both banks, each touching the next. Boys like Abdullah, here to shout for their house colors, called jokes back and forth. They even walked from boat to boat on the seats, to visit.

Hafiz was so excited he couldn't talk at first. He forgot about his shoes. He took his hand out of his pocket so he could clap, as the big boys did.

The racing boats began to collect around the starting line. A fresh wind blew little waves across the course. Abdullah said that would make the racing harder, but more fun.

On the opposite bank next to the starter, under the big school flag at the end of the rope, the band had a large boat to themselves. Underneath the noise of the crowd Hafiz could hear them tootling their horns and getting ready to play.

Suddenly everybody stood up. Hafiz did, too, holding onto Abdullah's coat. He wondered why they were standing. Then across the water there was music, a foreign tune. The little boy did not know that he was hearing "God Save the King" for the first time. He liked the sound, though it was so different from his favorite, the well-song.

Then the crowd sat down again, and from the starter's skiff there was a puff of smoke. Hafiz yelled with the others. The first race had begun.

It was to be a straightaway, warming-up affair. Four boats were entered. Only one could win! Hafiz' heart beat fast. In the second boat all the boys wore blue jerseys. Hafiz liked that color. It was the same as the sky at night above Solomon's Mountain, just before the first star shone.

As the boats passed them, Hafiz saw for an instant only the face of the boy in the second one who sat with his back to the goal. He was shouting at his crew, urging them on. It was Yusuf, Abdullah's friend who had come on the day when Hafiz fell in the water. His boat must win!

The four grew smaller as they hurtled down the course. Then they were all in a bunch as they rounded the racemaster's station, out in the basin at the halfway point. When they came nearer again, up the course to the finish, the second boat was gaining! The yelling swelled until it seemed like one big voice. Abdullah was yelling with all the others. Hafiz stood up again and tugged at his coat.

"Row, Yusuf Ali! Bring in the blue!" the boys were shouting, over and over.

Hafiz wondered how he could hear them. Yusuf leaned toward his paddlers. He held out his hands to them, pleading, urging. The paddles scarcely seemed to come out of the water, they came so fast. The other boats began to fall back. Now the second one was ahead, only a little. In another long breath the race was over. Yusuf had brought his boat in! There it went, first over the line, under the Kashmir colors in the very middle.

"I liked it," said Hafiz. He clapped his hands.

Abdullah was still whistling shrilly. All the visitors around them raised their paddles. It was a salute to the winning boat.

Abdullah leaned down to hear what Hafiz said. "I know that big boy," Hafiz told him, clapping again. "I am glad he won!"

Above the continuing noise Abdullah shouted, "You remembered Yusuf? Good boy! He is the coxswain. He steers the boat and leads the rowers. That was my house crew. They won that race!"

The long racing shells came next. These boys used real oars with squared ends. They sent their light craft scooting along the top of the water like a new sort of water bug. The whistling and the paddle salute came from the other bank at the end of that race. When the winning shell went over the finish line, all the crew raised their oars, too, straight up, like trees.

Hafiz clapped with the opposite bank, until

Abdullah said, "Sshh!" and made him sit down.

"That wasn't my house," Abdullah explained.

"But it was a beautiful race," Hafiz objected.

Abdullah said, "They are all beautiful, but the best are won by your own house. I didn't bring you along to shout for the other side!"

He laughed, so Hafiz knew he didn't mind really. But after that he watched Abdullah and clapped his hands and yelled only when he did. If he, Hafiz, could go to school, he wondered if he would be in that same mysterious "house" that Abdullah talked about.

In the next race they used heavier, bigger boats. All the crews had changed to swimming trunks. Ah, there was Yusuf again, with blue stripes on his trunks. Almost while Hafiz was telling himself this, the boys in Yusuf's boat were leaping into the water and their boat turned over. The crowd yelled, but nobody offered to help them!

Hafiz begged Abdullah to go out and get Yusuf. But the big brother was yelling so loud he did not hear. The boys swam along in the water, turned their boat right side up, and got in again, to go on with the race as if nothing had happened.

But it had happened, and Hafiz was scarcely breathing easily again when the next boat and the next keeled over in the same way. There was a great deal of churning water and splashing and noise.

"What did you think of that, Small One?"

Hafiz was very still.

"It is all right to shout for these boys. They are very brave!"

"But I was afraid they couldn't get out of the water!" Hafiz' voice sounded scared.

"But they do it on purpose! They like doing it! They have done it so many times they have lost count."

Hafiz did not seem convinced.

"It is part of the race," Abdullah went on. "They try to see how fast they can turn the boat over, get in again, and finish the course," he insisted.

"But I shouldn't like to do it," Hafiz said. His hands lay open, palms up, on his knees. His knees shook. Abdullah was sorry. He remembered something. Only two days before the little brother had confided his secret saving so that he, too, could go to school. What was he thinking?

Abdullah said aloud, "Here, come and stand between my knees, so you can see better. I will hold you. And don't worry about these chaps! Only the big boys do it. You never saw me do it, but I can! These are the ones who dive from the top of the school into the river every morning. They know how. They like it!"

Hafiz stood up willingly. Abdullah was right, he could see better. And his knees didn't shake any more.

"Does Yusuf dive?"

"I have seen him do it dozens of times. Some day you shall see him, too. Yusuf does everything well."

"But not any better than you, Abdullah," Hafiz insisted. "I know that thing."

He knew too, now, why Abdullah could leap aboard the *doonga*. They did teach it at that school. Could he . . . ?

Another race was beginning. This was for smaller boys, in lighter boats. The little oarsmen were not much bigger than Hafiz. They sat as easily as if they were a part of the boat. Hafiz began to feel he might like to do it, after all.

There were several other races before the afternoon ended, but the one Hafiz talked most about when they reached the *doonga* again was the handicap race. That, and seeing Yusuf.

He would remember their second meeting for a long time. On the way home, the boat in which Yusuf was returning had passed them. It had pulled up so that Yusuf and Abdullah could talk. After a while Yusuf said, "Isn't this your little brother who fell in the lake?" And Abdullah had answered proudly, "Yes, this is my Hafiz!" How glad Hafiz was that he was wearing the new green shoes! He hoped Yusuf had noticed them. But more than that, Yusuf had put his hand on Hafiz' shoulder and said, "Who knows? Perhaps one day you, too, shall belong to the Blues!"

In the cooking place at bedtime, Hafiz told it all to Rafia. He sat cross-legged on his mat and wore his old cap again.

"Those boys, Rafia, those big boys," he said, "they fell into the water on purpose! They made the boat turn over!" His eyes grew bigger at the memory. "I thought Yusuf would surely be hurt, but Abdullah laughed."

"What happened after that?"

Rafia knew. She had heard the story through several times since Hafiz had returned. But if he wanted to live it over again, she could listen. Her day's work was finished. She had her knitting and felt as comfortable as Hafiz looked.

"There was much noise. The band blew horns and the boys on the bank yelled. The boys in the water got back in their boats and went on with the race. Why did they make the boat turn over, Rafia?"

Rafia tossed her braids back. Even a girl could answer that question.

"They were just showing off, little brother! They call it being brave. They weren't afraid

225

to go in the water, so they went in. That was to show everybody that they were brave."

"I wonder if they teach boys how to be brave at that school. I am not brave, Rafia. My knees shook."

Rafia laid her knitting down. She needed both hands to talk just then. She wagged one finger, the pointing finger, in time with her words. It was very like her mother.

"Hafiz, look at me!"

He did so, in surprise. Her tone was different somehow.

"Hear my words! I, a daughter of the faith, say this thing. Do not ever tell me again that you are not a brave boy. You were brave the day you fell in the lake. You were brave when you told that you, and only you, had put the baby on the Sahib's bed."

"But, Rafia . . . !"

"Nay, hear me out! Nobody teaches boys to

be brave. It is in you. You are, or you are not. I have spoken. I say you are a brave boy now."

She picked up her knitting. They sat quietly, not even hearing the night sounds outside.

Although his sister's words seemed right, Hafiz was still a little doubtful. How did Rafia know?

"But my knees shook, Rafia!" he argued.

"No matter! They may shake again some day, but you will do what you have to do. And you do not need to go to school to learn how."

It certainly made Hafiz feel easier in his heart. But Rafia was a girl. How could she know about school?

15

A DIFFERENT RACE IS RUN

IN THE CHANNEL WHERE THE *DOONGA* AND
the houseboat lay, the willow shade grew thick
in early June, making a cool retreat when the
midday sun grew warm.

Summer beauty lay all around. The cherry
boats were heaped high with rosy fruit. In the
marshes water lilies were spreading their great

green leaves, where dewdrops lay in the morning like giant's tears. Later there would be pink buds and wide, goldenhearted blossoms lying among the pads. Hafiz could remember what fun it had been the summer before, to tug at a tough stem and have three or four hollow rubbery feet of it come away in his hand.

The marsh hens and dabchicks proudly led their new families in and out of the grasses. The ducks had eight downy ducklings, which Hafiz discovered one morning when he went out to see if the little boats were all right.

The yellow babies were twittering and peeping about in the water, kicking vigorously after their mother. What joy it would be to hold one! It seemed easy to catch one, but he found he could not go near. The old drake hissed, and the rest of the big ducks made such a fuss and chatter that he had to give it up. Perhaps Abdullah could get it for him.

The week following the races had been very quiet for Hafiz. He still had the red ball. The Sahib had said to leave that for him. But Hafiz had discovered that more fun was to be had with the ball if two played.

Abdullah was out in the *shikara* every day and the others were too busy. Firewood to be chopped, the rice-husking, mending, visiting with passing friends, the water-pipe and the cooking, kept the family active all day long. All but Hafiz. The little boy tagged Rafia until even she grew tired of hearing about Yusuf and boat racing. And Hafiz began to think her housekeeping was dull business.

Now, here were the new baby ducks! If only he could catch one!

Abdullah and the Sahib came back in mid-morning, and the Sahib went up on his roof deck to work on a picture. Hafiz hurried into the cooking place.

His brother sat by one of the open spaces in the frame where the mat was rolled up. He was drinking cold tea and giving his mother the latest Valley news. He and the Sahib had been in the city and he had stopped at the wood-carver's. June is the marriage month and there was much to tell.

When Hafiz appeared, Abdullah said, "I saw Yusuf in the bazaar. He sent his salaams to you!"

Hafiz' eyes glowed. "Salaams for me?" He wanted to hear the words again.

"For you! Who else does he know in this family?"

"He knows me!" said Hafiz, proudly.

The talk went on again and Hafiz listened. He would wait until the tea was finished before asking for help with the baby duck.

Abdullah sat there shaking his head as soon as he realized what Hafiz meant. He set down the empty tea mug.

"Don't go near those ducks, Hafiz! They belong to the farmer, and if anything happens, pfft! he will make trouble." Abdullah was suddenly very stern.

"But how could it make trouble if I hold just one?" Hafiz argued.

Abdullah tried again. "You might hurt it, and then he would want money again! Even if you did not hurt it, he likes making trouble, and that would be a fine reason."

Hafiz sulked. So he couldn't play with the ducks! That old farmer! He wandered back to the willow root. He kicked the tree and a few yellow leaves floated down. The water was so still they stayed where they fell. He sat down on the root and looked at the little boats.

Then he remembered the message from Yusuf. He smiled. That nice big boy! The race was still easy to remember in each detail. Suddenly he sprang up and clapped his hands. Why not have a little race like that big one? His boats would get very wet if any of them turned over, but he could dry them again.

It took rather a long time to arrange everything. He untied the little boats and lined them up, changing their position several times until it satisfied him. He checked his money. It was safe. Should he put the *Silver Moon* in the race? The school had not entered pleasure boats in its races. It would make one more in the lineup, he decided, so the *Silver Moon* was set carefully back in the water.

He had to make one trip to the *doonga*, to get string from Rafia. She was a long time finding what he wanted. But the stores box, that wonderful treasure chest, had some rough hemp stuff from the rice bags. He showed her where to cut and she separated it for him, in several unequal pieces.

Back at the willow root, the little boats were tied by their red painters to the hemp lengths. These were fastened in a row to the long stick. His race course would have to be all in one direction, but the stretch of water by the runway would be all right.

When everything was ready, and he stood with the long stick in his hand to pull the boats through the water, he realized one thing was missing. The water was too still. The other race course at Gagribal had been a little rough. Abdullah had said the race would be more fun to watch because the water was not smooth.

While Hafiz was searching for a good branch, one with leaves on it, to whip up some waves, Abdullah came along the runway. He was dressed in his white table coat. That meant it was almost time to serve the Sahib's food.

Hafiz showed him the little ducks and Abdullah repeated his warning. "Mind what I said, Hafiz! Let the ducks alone! I have seen the farmer. He is working up there in his field today."

"I am having a boat race, Abdullah. See, this is for waves! I won't bother the ducks."

A fine switch of willow hung from a low branch. The leaves were thick and long. They ought to make splendid waves.

Hafiz was still twisting away, trying to break it off, when Abdullah went back to the *doonga*. It was not long before the Sahib shouted from the roof deck for his lunch.

By that time Hafiz had the willow switch in his hand. He began to yell and beat the water with it. The quiet little channel suddenly broke into all the reality of a big race. Hafiz had not counted on the ducks' help with the noise part. The willow leaves did make wonderful waves, and he started to pull the little boats through the choppy water.

The ducks were thoroughly aroused. The old drake hissed and all the big ducks swam angrily about. The peeping ducklings huddled around their mother. Suddenly one of the other ducks darted toward the little boats. Hafiz saw it coming, but he was not fast enough. The duck opened wide its yellow bill and scooped up the nearest boat. It was the *Silver Moon*.

Hafiz screamed and began to run on the path. But the duck made for the open water beyond the runway. The string broke.

Abdullah was coming from the cooking place with a covered dish of food in his hand, for the Sahib's lunch.

Hafiz ran toward him. "Abdullah, the duck has my boat! My *Silver Moon!* Get it, Abdullah! Look, there it goes! Out in the lake. Oh! Oh! Abdullah, I want my boat!" The frantic little boy was sobbing.

Abdullah had seen. He set the dish of food

down in the path, ran aboard the *doonga,* and loosed the painter of the *shikara.* Hafiz was at his heels. They followed the duck, which was heading now toward the marsh. The farmer could be heard, shouting from his field.

"Ai! Hai!" Abdullah groaned. "That was the farmer. Now there will be a do!"

They were gaining on the duck. Hafiz forgot to be afraid. He leaned out over the water and tried to snatch the precious *shikara* from the duck's bill. But all he got was a handful of tail feathers. The feathers scattered over the water. Abdullah paddled a little faster.

The duck quacked once, and very loud, when the feathers came out, and dropped the *shikara.* It floated in reach and Hafiz scooped it up. He bent over the precious boat. The little seat had slid open and the coins were gone.

"My fees!" he cried, with the tears pouring down his dirty face. "My school fees! They are gone! All my money!" He did not mind now that his hiding place would be known. "I didn't bother the duck, Abdullah! Why did it take my boat?"

"Perhaps it was hungry. Don't cry, my Small One!" Abdullah was panting, he was paddling so hard. "I saw . . . the thing. It is . . . that you need a . . . better place to play. Never mind! Let us get the duck back, for . . . the farmer. That will help! Ai! There it goes!"

Abdullah's lips closed in a thin line. He meant to get that duck. He did get it! At the edge of the marsh the bird tried to slip into the reeds, but Abdullah rested his paddle and reached for it. He got a firm grip on what was left of the tail. More feathers came out. The duck quacked and struggled, but Abdullah landed it in the bottom of the *shikara*. He had won that race!

He sat quite still for a minute, getting his

breath. He held the duck with one hand, while he wiped Hafiz' face with the tail of his shirt. The dirt and the tears came off in a black streak.

"Don't cry, Small One!" he said again. "Never mind the fees! Here is the duck!" He held the helpless bird up by the feet and it quacked. "What a sight, a duck without a tail!" Hafiz laughed. It did look funny.

Abdullah pushed the boat away from the reeds and turned it about. Hafiz' tears started again when he had to lay the *Silver Moon* down to take charge of the flapping duck. That took both hands. He sobbed all the way back to the *doonga,* and the duck quacked.

Rafia and her father and mother were standing quietly, waiting for them. The farmer was sitting in his boat alongside. He was not quiet. He began shouting at them as soon as they came in hearing distance.

"Give me my duck!" he demanded. "I saw the whole thing. It isn't enough that you steal babies, you take my food too! I saw you chasing my duck!"

Abdullah drew the boats together. He took the duck from Hafiz' hands and offered it to the farmer. The farmer pushed it away.

"No, I don't want it. I won't have it. You have spoiled it. You will pay me for this act. One of my best birds! Who wants a duck without a tail? I will be laughed at. You can give me money. But a duck without a tail I will not have."

"There is nothing wrong with the duck. What is the loss of a few feathers? Take your bird and stop making a nuisance of yourself!" Abdullah tried some of his big, school words, but they did not impress the farmer.

"I lost more than feathers," Hafiz began, "I lost . . ." But Abdullah put his hand on

Hafiz' mouth when the farmer was not looking.

"Don't tell about your rupee, Hafiz! He will never go!"

Abdullah's warning was just in time. The farmer had not heard.

"I do not want the duck. I will take money now."

When Abdullah flung out empty hands in a familiar gesture, the farmer laughed, scornfully.

"You have it. You also have a tenant. Let him pay!"

"I will pay!" said a quiet voice, and there was the Sahib, standing at the railing of his roof deck.

There was a sudden and complete silence. How much had he heard? Abdullah thought guiltily of the food, cold now, and waiting in the path. This was truly a patient Sahib!

"Row over here!" the quiet voice insisted.

The farmer obeyed, until his boat was directly beneath the spot where the Sahib stood.

"How much do you charge for a duck with no tail?"

"One rupee!" the farmer answered promptly.

Something shone in the air, and there was the jingling, ringing sound of metal. The man scrambled around in the bottom of the boat, picking it up. He flipped the money with his thumb and forefinger to see if it were good.

"Now then," the quiet voice went on. "Go! And if I catch you bothering these people again this season, I shall report you to the police! You and your sneaking lies . . . yes, and Sayyad Khan, too! Tell him that for me!"

The farmer started to say something, but the Sahib would not let him speak. And if ever a man rowing a boat could be said to crawl, the farmer crawled humbly away from that place.

"I hope he is satisfied now," said Abdullah. "He has got a rupee at last."

When the man was out of sight round the bend, the Sahib called to Abdullah.

"Cook the duck for my dinner tonight. It will have an uncommon fine taste, I think."

While the delayed luncheon was served, the rest of the family heard Hafiz' story. He showed the *Silver Moon* and the little sliding seat which the grandfather had so cleverly planned.

"All gone," said the little boy, his voice shaking, "all my fees."

His mother tried to soothe him. "Have I not told thee one wise one in the family is enough? Do not think any more of the school! You will not need the rupee. And you still have the lucky piece!"

In the soft comfort of his mother's arms,

Hafiz felt for the lump in his pocket seam. Yes, there it was! He had quite forgot it. He could start his savings over again!

Abdullah brought a message when his work was finished.

"The Sahib is sending salaams, and wishes to see thee, my father," he said.

16

THE SAHIB MAKES A BARGAIN

THE DUCK WAS YOUNG AND TENDER AND
made a fine dish for dinner. But long before it
was eaten Hafiz had good reason to believe it
a very wonderful duck, indeed.

The father was still talking with the Sahib
up on the roof deck. Hafiz had gone back to his

245

boats, untying them from the stick and clear-
ing up after the interrupted race.

Abdullah came to him at the willow root.
The big brother did not say anything at first.
But he held in his fingers, so that Hafiz could
see, a shining silver rupee.

"Did you lose this?" he asked.

Hafiz was not certain that Abdullah, in spite
of all that had happened, was not again having
fun. So he began his answer cautiously.

"There was once a rupee . . ." and Abdullah finished for him, "which I found at housecleaning time."

"Yes," Hafiz went on, "and I hid it in my
shikara, and a duck stole the *shikara* and ate the
rupee."

Abdullah took up the tale. "And the Sahib
bought the duck from the farmer and had it
cooked for dinner and the rupee was found."

The little boy's eyes sparkled with delight.

"Oh, Abdullah! Is it that rupee? Is it mine? Did the duck really swallow my money? Is it truly my found rupee?"

Abdullah wagged his head up and down in the same way Hafiz often did. "It truly is," said he.

They were still laughing when the father came along the path. His eyes smiled, but his face was very solemn.

"Come along, my sons, with me," he said.

They looked at each other questioningly, and followed him to the *doonga*. Hafiz slipped his hand into Abdullah's. There was something strange that he did not understand.

The father gathered the family around him. Rafia brought the pipe but he waved it away. There was a little silence. He did not know how to begin.

"The Sahib says," he began finally, "that there has been a great deal of noise in this place,

247

this season. Too much noise!" He looked round, still solemnly, at his only daughter, that quietest member of the family.

"The farmer made some of it," said Hafiz quickly.

His father pretended not to hear. "The Sahib says," he continued, "that boys should learn useful work."

"I work," cried Hafiz again. "I carried books . . . I held the boat when the Sahib came. I go with Abdullah in the boat . . . when he lets me."

"Peace!" said the father. "Hear me!" He rumbled and hurrumphed, down in his beard. "And so, the Sahib says, if I will let my younger son go to school, he will pay the fees."

The big man's eyes were kind as he looked at Hafiz. "He said it would be worth it!" he added.

Hafiz let out his breath in a long sigh. He did

not realize he had been holding it. Now he knew his father had been having fun, the way Abdullah did.

"The fees of the River School, my son!" said the father, nodding at Hafiz. "Not the shouting one in the bazaar!"

There was silence once more, but only for a moment, in the cooking place. Then the mother began to cry.

"Hush, woman!" said the father sternly. "See this thing as it is! First, the fees will be paid. There will be no debt for them to Sayyad Khan." He bent down one big finger.

The mother was crying into the end of her scarf, but he went on with the finger business. "Second! If next year is a good season for boats, there can be Rafia's engagement! It is high time!" Another finger joined the first, and the mother came out from behind the scarf. "Third!" He said the last thing louder. "This boy cannot stay a baby forever!"

Hafiz got up and stood beside his mother. It was now his part to comfort her.

"Yes, my mother, I am a man now! Said I not so when I carried the books? There is that wood-carver baby called Hafiz. They will let you borrow him in my place sometimes." He patted her shoulder. "I should go now and give salaams to the Sahib for this thing."

He marched out, his back very straight. The two green shoes of Kashmir leather made one step to the door, two steps to the plank, and two to the runway. The baby Hafiz was gone.

It was evening again under the willow tree. Hafiz finished tying the little boats securely in their place under the high-arching root. He sat back on his heels to look at them. The newest one, the little *shikara*, was fastened to the small *doonga*. The *Silver Moon* would never be the same again, but it still rode evenly in the water.

Far across the valley, Hafiz could see the shining snows. They were gold at the top where the sun was setting. They had looked like that all summer, bright at evening time, as if they had been dusted with yellow curry powder from the spice merchant's shop in the bazaar.

A boat went by in the channel beyond the houseboat. It sent little waves lapping against the runway. The waves came into the quiet garden backwater and the little fleet rocked and knocked together.

There was a music box playing on the passing boat. Hafiz could hear the tune for some time after it had gone by. He wondered if there would be music at the school. Ah, yes, he remembered the band at the races.

After a while the little boats swung more gently again by their faded red painters. They would stay that way tomorrow and tomorrow and many tomorrows. Hafiz was going to school on the river. He would learn how to do the useful work the Sahib had talked about. He would jump on boats and dive, and perhaps they would let him play in the band.

Rafia peered out into the shadows and called him.

"Bedtime for schoolboys!" she said.

Hafiz chuckled way down in his tummy, and ran to her.

A little wind stirred the willow tree. A few yellowing leaves dropped down on the tiny boats. The days of Hafiz' playtime were over for this summer. Tomorrow he was going to school.